the further adventures of
SHERLOCK HOLMES

THE STALWART COMPANIONS

D0063848

AVAILABLE NOW FROM TITAN BOOKS

THE FURTHER ADVENTURES OF SHERLOCK HOLMES
THE ECTOPLASMIC MAN
Daniel Stashower
ISBN: 9781848564923

THE FURTHER ADVENTURES OF SHERLOCK HOLMES
THE MAN FROM HELL
Barrie Roberts
ISBN: 9781848565081

THE FURTHER ADVENTURES OF SHERLOCK HOLMES
THE SCROLL OF THE DEAD
David Stuart Davies
ISBN: 9781848564930

THE FURTHER ADVENTURES OF SHERLOCK HOLMES
THE VEILED DETECTIVE
David Stuart Davies
ISBN: 9781848564909

THE FURTHER ADVENTURES OF SHERLOCK HOLMES
THE WAR OF THE WORLDS
Manly W. Wellman & Wade Wellman
ISBN: 9781848564916

THE STALWART COMPANIONS

H. PAUL JEFFERS

TITAN BOOKS

THE FURTHER ADVENTURES OF SHERLOCK HOLMES
THE STALWART COMPANIONS

ISBN: 9781848565098

Published by
Titan Books
A division of Titan Publishing Group Ltd
144 Southwark St
London
SE1 0UP

First edition: February 2010
10 9 8 7 6 5 4 3 2 1

© 1978, 2010 H. Paul Jeffers

Visit our website:
www.titanbooks.com

What did you think of this book? We love to hear from our readers.
Please email us at: readerfeedback@titanemail.com, or write to us at
the above address. To receive advance information, news,
competitions, and exclusive Titan offers online, please register as a
member by clicking the 'sign up' button on our website:
www.titanbooks.com

A CIP catalogue record for this title is available from the British Library.

Printed in the USA.

*This book is dedicated to
three stalwart companions:*

Gary, Rose Ann and Sid.

Foreword

B y no definition had I ever considered myself a serious student of the life, times, cases and adventures of Mr Sherlock Holmes of 221B Baker Street. Although I had read the Holmes stories, I considered him nothing more than the fictional creation of Sir Arthur Conan Doyle, dismissing with alacrity the various propositions that Holmes and his biographer, Dr John H. Watson, had been historical personalities and that Doyle was, at best, Watson's literary agent.

As a journalist, I found these theories of a real Holmes amusing while admiring the inventiveness of the authors.

Lately, however, manuscripts purporting to be 'lost' Watson writings have been turning up with great regularity and finding their way into print, each of them pretending to fill in certain gaps in the literature of the sleuth of Baker Street.

Whether or not these surfacing Watsonian latter-day publications are genuine Watson, I could not say, though a special friend of mine who is regarded as an expert on Holmes has expressed grave doubts about their authenticity. I leave the disposition of that problem to the experts. What I no longer leave to speculation is the question of whether Holmes walked this earth with other men. I know he did.

It is ironic that I, the sceptic, stumbled onto the proof that Holmes was not only a real person but had engaged in a collaboration with a young man who was destined to become the Twenty-sixth President of the United States. This singular companionship resulted in the unearthing of one of the most dastardly conspiracies in the annals of American history, the details of which are revealed for the first time in this publication.

In editing this historic material, I have been mindful of the doubts that will plague the reader on every page, so I have included notes and other material which I believe demonstrate, through independent research, the veracity of the text. In keeping with this purpose of providing independent data to support the text, I have included an introduction, giving the details of the unearthing of the startling collaboration between the world's first consulting detective and the young Theodore Roosevelt. In Notes and an afterword, I offer explanations that are possible as to why this amazing information has not been revealed before now. I have tried to verify the facts as stated in the text where that data is verifiable – such as dates, places, and descriptions of places, events, and personalities – to see if it could have been possible for Holmes and Roosevelt to have known each other in New York City in the summer of 1880, and to collaborate on an important criminal investigation of such a sensitive nature that it could not be published during their lifetimes.

Unfortunately, had the case been publicised at the time, one of the tragedies of American history might have been averted.

H. Paul Jeffers

New York City, 1978

Introduction

ᘒ

Fifteen years before Theodore Roosevelt took on the job of President of the Board of Police Commissioners of the New York Police Department, he learned a lesson in the fine art of criminology from the greatest detective of all time, though each man was, at the time, still in his twenties. One need only look into the exceptional job which Roosevelt did as Police Commissioner to realise that he had acquired very progressive views on how a police department should function and that he had developed a very keen sense of the value of the methods of crime detection pioneered by Sherlock Holmes. This Roosevelt record as head of a metropolitan police force bears the unmistakable imprint of his great teacher. In a memoir of his days as head of the NYPD, Roosevelt wrote, "The first duty of the true democrat, of the man really loyal to the principles of popular government, is to see that law is enforced and order upheld." It would be hard to find any sentiment more Sherlockian.

Nearly a century has passed since Roosevelt and Holmes joined hands to investigate a crime which the young Roosevelt, a habitual diarist, recorded in great detail and at length. It is this record by Roosevelt which makes up the bulk of this publication. The importance of this document cannot be underestimated, for it is the only known account of a Sherlock Holmes case not recorded by either Watson or Holmes and, therefore, is evidence of a historical Holmes.

In the course of the investigation which uncovered the existence of the long, affectionate, and productive friendship between Sherlock Holmes and Theodore Roosevelt, I had the benefit of the expertise and counsel of one of the authorities on Sherlockiana, my dear friend and personal adviser B. Alexander Wiggins. Member of the Baker Street Irregulars since his adolescence; author of innumerable articles, essays, and monographs on Holmes; and technical adviser to publishers, film producers, and authors, "Wiggy" was one of the most ardent proponents of the proposition that Holmes had been a real person. Further, he claimed to be the grandson of the same Wiggins who was the leader of that pack of street urchins, the original Baker Street Irregulars, who proved useful to Holmes in several cases. A giant of a man, Wiggy resided in Greenwich Village while teaching at New York University. His lodgings were evocative of the rooms shared by Holmes and Watson, those legendary digs on the second floor of 221B Baker Street. Cluttered with books, newspapers, magazines, and artefacts of every description having to do with Holmes, the flat had become world famous as an address where a researcher on any aspect of the world's first consulting detective could find answers, either directly from a vast library on the subject or from the expert's memory trove. Seated in a spacious armchair at the center of his Holmesian archives, Wiggy resembled a Buddha, an immense dressing gown over his scarlet pajamas, his feet in a pair of ornate Persian slippers, a collection of pipes at hand on the table beside the chair. From this spot, Wiggy rarely stirred, conducting his business by phone, letter, or telegram and, when it was necessary to do business in person, holding 'court' as the world came to him. The persons who came for his advice or assistance paid handsomely. A small number of persons had the good fortune to have engaged him as a literary agent.

It was not necessary to be a devotee of Holmes to come under the literary wing of B. Alexander Wiggins, but it was nearly impossible to have any kind of conversation with him without hearing quotations, maxims, anecdotes, and instructive examples from 'the canon' in the course of it. As in the case of the man he had devoted his life to studying, Wiggy was a brilliant reasoner, a persuasive debater. More, he was a tenacious evangelist on the subject of a historical Holmes. (This was what brought me into the life of B. Alexander Wiggins in my role as a journalist assigned by a magazine editor to interview the man reputed to know as much about Holmes as Conan Doyle himself, possibly more.) My incredulity regarding a real-life Holmes fired Wiggins' proselytising spirit. "Holmes not only lived," he informed me emphatically, "but he lived to the ripe old age of one hundred and three years!"

"Then why have I not been able to read historical accounts of his life and adventures?"

"But you can! Watson!"

"You mean Conan Doyle."

With a wave of his huge hand, he dismissed my impertinence. "Conan Doyle was never more than a peddler of other people's writings!"

"I know of no instance in which a newspaper provided independent evidence of the existence of one Sherlock Holmes."

"Holmes avoided publicity sedulously. As Watson wrote, Holmes' nature 'was always averse to anything in the shape of public applause.' So, it is no wonder that the London papers have no accounts of him. Holmes was careful to let the credit for the resolution of problems go to the officers from Scotland Yard. Nor did Holmes' adventures in the

United States ever make it into the American press. But it is a fact that he was here and that he solved at least two mysteries. In January 1880 he solved a problem for the Vanderbilt family. Later, in July, there was the awful affair in Baltimore concerning the Abernetty family."

"Despite Holmes' desire for anonymity, I cannot imagine the newspapers of America in that period permitting the famous Sherlock Holmes of 221B Baker Street to arrive in this country without making note of it in the news columns," I stated.

"In the first place," replied Wiggy, "Holmes came here when he was in the earliest period of his career. In 1879, Holmes was twenty-six years of age. He had yet to meet Watson, yet to take up residence at 221-B (he was residing on Montague Street at the time), yet to enjoy a reputation outside the smallest circles of law enforcement. Secondly, he came here incognito, using his stage name. If you wish to find references to Holmes in musty old news columns you must look for the name William Escott, which is the name he used while acting. It's a clever derivation of his Christian names, William S. (for Sherlock) Scott."

"My interest in old newspapers is crime news," I stated, referring to a current project – a history of crime news in New York City, which I was researching painstakingly in microfilmed archives of New York newspapers. This work I conducted in the quiet of the fourth floor research room of the Mid-Manhattan Branch of the New York Public Library on Fortieth Street just off Fifth Avenue. For months, every spare hour in my schedule was spent before the viewing screens of the microfilm readers, studying the accounts of crimes, great and small, as recorded by *The New York Times*. By the end of June 1977, I had progressed in my research to the first half of 1880.

An account of a murder in the Gramercy Park area caught my attention. It seemed to be a common street crime, but one paragraph in the story lifted this piece of journalism above routine:

Detective Wilson Hargreave was summoned urgently to the scene of the horrible event from a private dinner at the Fifty-seventh Street home of Mr T. Roosevelt, recently graduated from Harvard. The police official and Mr Roosevelt had attended a performance of Shakespeare's *Twelfth Night* at the Union Square Theatre and were in the company of a member of the acting company, Mr William Escott. All three men were active at the scene of the murder.

Riveted to my chair, I read the article again and again, fascinated by the presence of the name "William Escott." After making a photocopy of the item, I rushed to Wiggy's house. "Is it possible," I asked, "that Holmes and Roosevelt knew each other?"

"If you eliminate the impossible, what is left, no matter how improbable, is the truth," Wiggy said. He took down from his shelves an array of reference books and pored over them until, at last, he leaned back in his chair and announced, "Yes."

"Yes, what?"

"It is probable."

"*What* is probable?"

"That Holmes and Roosevelt knew each other and that they worked together in the solving of this Gramercy Park murder."

"Now how the hell do you know that?" I groaned.

"Through a combination of research into the facts and a little deduction based on the facts. Permit me to explain. That these men were present at the Gramercy Park murder scene is known, given the tangible evidence of this newspaper account and the paper's reputation for accuracy. The questions which one might honestly raise are these: 1) What was Roosevelt doing in Manhattan? 2) Why was he in the company of Mr Hargreave and Mr Escott? 3) Why did Hargreave take Roosevelt and Escott to the scene of a crime? 4) Was William Escott, in fact, Sherlock Holmes?"

"And the answers?" I asked, settling back in a chair.

"Roosevelt was in Manhattan because he lived here. He had just graduated from Harvard and was stopping at his home prior to leaving for a tour of the West with his brother. I know this from the sketch in this volume of biographies of American Presidents. This sketch also notes that while at Harvard Mr Roosevelt devoted himself to a study of science, and it is from this information that we may deduce that Roosevelt knew of the work of Mr Sherlock Holmes, had arranged to meet Holmes during his run in New York with the Shakespearean troupe and had taken steps to bring Holmes and Hargreave together for dinner after the performance of *Twelfth Night*. Finally, Holmes took an active part in the resolution of the Gramercy Park murder case. I see a quizzical look on your face. Pray, listen. It's very elementary. Holmes had invited Roosevelt to the performance of *Twelfth Night*. I state this on the basis of my deduction that the two young men already had an acquaintanceship, probably by correspondence. We know Roosevelt was interested in science. That interest surely would have impelled him to read Holmes' monographs on tobaccos, identifying footprints, and the dating of documents. In this correspondence, Holmes, of course, would have informed young Roosevelt that he would be in America as the actor William Escott and would have expressed a desire to meet Roosevelt. This Holmes arranged by the simple device of sending Roosevelt a pair of tickets to a performance of the play that would coincide with Roosevelt's return to Manhattan after graduation."

"Why a pair of tickets?" I asked. "Why not one?"

"Well, it would be common courtesy to send two tickets, wouldn't it? Besides, we know that Roosevelt attended the theatre with Hargreave."

"Perhaps Hargreave invited Roosevelt?"

"That is possible but not probable. No, I expect that Roosevelt, having gotten the tickets and having wondered whom to take to the theatre with him, invited the detective with the intention of introducing him to Holmes and bringing the two men together for an evening of fascinating conversation. This assumes that Roosevelt already had an interest in the art of detection, although it would be some years before he would, himself, be the commissioner of police in New York City."

"Very pat," I smiled, "but it all hinges on whether Holmes was in fact Escott."

"That is beyond question because it stretches the laws of coincidence to believe that an actor with the same name we know Holmes used on the stage would find himself in the company of a scion of one of New York's best families *and* in company with Roosevelt and Hargreave at the scene of a major crime. That coincidence disposed of, we know from Holmes' biographers that he was in America at this time, having arrived here aboard the White Star liner Empress Queen in the first week of December 1879 as a member of the Sasanoff Shakespearean Company as William Escott."

"Why didn't Holmes identify himself with his true name to the reporter?"

"Surely, you know by now that Holmes would never do that!"

"Why would Hargreave drag along these two young men to the scene of a crime?"

Wiggy chuckled, his great torso quaking with amusement. "Can you really doubt that an ambitious detective would pass up the chance to consult with a man whom he knew to be, already, one of the most brilliant criminal investigators in history?"

"Incredible!"

"Logical!" And precisely what young Mr Roosevelt would have suggested had not Hargreave first invited Holmes to visit the scene of the crime. It is interesting to know that as early as 1880, fifteen years before he became commissioner, Roosevelt was impressed with Holmes and willing to consult him. It now convinces me that the coincidence of two later dates in the lives of both men is to be considered significant."

"I miss the point, I'm afraid."

"In the data we have about Sherlock Holmes there is a period known as the 'missing year.' From late 1895 to late 1896 there is no word in the literature on the exact whereabouts of Holmes and what he was working on. I now believe that Holmes was in America, because it was in 1895 that Teddy Roosevelt took on the job as police commissioner. I am certain that Holmes would not have hesitated to come to the assistance of his old friend, if asked, and we can see from this Gramercy Park affair that Roosevelt had witnessed the effect of calling upon Holmes in criminal cases."

"You stated unequivocally that Holmes solved the Gramercy Park murder?"

"Indubitably."

"I will have to look up subsequent accounts of the investigation in the archives before I can grant you that."

"You will see I am right."

"Wild conjecture on your part."

"More than conjecture, I assure you. First, Holmes rarely failed to solve his cases. Second, because there is no record of this case before now, I deduce, because it turned into a matter of such importance, such delicacy, that Holmes took steps to see that it was never publicised as part of the record of his career. That means your job is not going to be easy."

"My job?"

"Surely you are going to follow up on this?"

"Well, I don't know, I—"

"God, man, think of it! Holmes and Teddy Roosevelt engaged in the solution of what we must assume was a crime with implications far beyond simple murder! I would be astounded if you did not dig into this affair."

"I wouldn't know where to begin."

"Nonsense. We begin with the Roosevelt archives."

"You believe Roosevelt kept a record of his association with Holmes?"

"Wouldn't you? I surely would have."

"I see your point."

"Precisely. Now we must confront the question of where to look for the evidence."

"Washington. Oyster Bay. The National Archives."

Shaking his head, Wiggy said, "I think not."

"Then where?"

"I would be very much surprised if we have to leave New York City to find what we're looking for. I believe it lies within the files of the New York Police Department. Logic dictates this conclusion. Would you agree that it makes sense for Roosevelt's papers concerning Holmes to be in his files dating from his years as head of the police department? I trust your contacts in the modern-day NYPD are of such stature that you will have no trouble getting us into the places where we are most likely to find what we seek."

In a taxi going downtown to the new police headquarters building, my friend was uncharacteristically animated because of his excitement at the prospect of uncovering, at last, direct evidence that Mr Sherlock Holmes had not been a mere fictional invention but was a living human being who had played a role in the career of one of America's giants, a fellow whom B. Alexander Wiggins had obviously come to know and respect as a result of his recent research into his career.

"A remarkable young man who has gotten short shrift in the literature of American Presidents," he remarked as our taxi careered through the streets. "I had a devil of a time finding biographical material beyond the superficial characterisation of the man as a hardy fellow who went around shouting, "Bully!" He was a robust man, of course, due entirely to his determination to overcome childhood weaknesses which had left him puny and subject to every kind of bullying. He developed his physique and became an excellent boxer. I thrill at the thought that he and Holmes, who was an excellent boxer, might have engaged in a few bouts. A crack shot, too. And a young man at college with an interest in scientific matters that could rival Holmes'. His life was fraught with personal tragedies. Did you know that his mother and his wife died on the *same day*? He rebounded from that double-barrelled disaster, however, just as he recouped from a humiliating defeat when he ran for mayor of New York in 1886. Came in *fourth*! His public career was never easy, not even when he was head of the police department. A very curious thing, that episode! William Strong, a reform mayor, picked Roosevelt to become commissioner of the corruption-ridden force, and T. R. accepted the challenge with relish. He fired the chief of the uniformed force, a rascal who had amassed three hundred thousand dollars in graft while in uniform. While commissioner, Roosevelt used to don a black cape and go out at night looking for crooked cops. A cape! Does that have a familiar ring to it? The newspapers loved him and there was talk about a bid for the White House. But then Mr Roosevelt learned that it is one thing to root out official corruption, quite another to tamper with the trivial illegalities of private individuals. He insisted on enforcing the Sunday Blue Laws by closing the saloons. Not long, and he was under great pressure to get out of office. He did, in 1897, to become Assistant Secretary of the Navy. Throughout this career, I am sure, he kept in close contact with a fellow across the Atlantic, whose own career was on the rise, Mr Sherlock Holmes."

"That's for the files to prove," I noted.

"They will, my friend," Wiggy grinned. "They will."

No reporter ventures into the archives of any police department without suspicion, but when it became known that I was interested in the annals and files from the last century, the New York Police Department accepted the fact that my poking around was no threat, and Wiggy and I were left undisturbed to go where the archives might lead us. "That was easier than I expected," laughed Wiggy as we descended deep into the bowels of headquarters.

"The power of the press," I muttered, sniffing the dry, dusty, cardboard smells of the huge storage room where the New York Police Department kept its past, its triumphs, its failures, its heroic tales and its skeletons.

Clapping his pudgy hands, Wiggy chuckled, "Ah, the game's afoot!"

Watching my bulky friend as he knelt and bent (not without difficulty) to peer at the faded, yellowing labels on the fronts of battered and sagging storage cartons, each one leading us farther back into history, I saw B. Alexander Wiggins as the personification of all Sherlockians who, as Vincent Starrett wrote, visualised Holmes with trusty Watson at his side, alive to those who love them well in a romantic chamber of the heart, in a nostalgic country of the mind where it is always 1895.

We, however, were looking for Holmes of a still earlier year – 1880.

"What have we here?" boomed the voice of B. Alexander Wiggins, sprawled on the dusty floor, moon-round face pressed close to a storage bin. "A pair of initials. T. R. Ha! My friend, we are on the trail!" Gently, tenderly, trembling with awe and anticipation, he drew the aged box into the dim light of bare bulbs from the ceiling above and carefully lifted its lid. Pausing before reaching into the half-empty box, Wiggy looked at me with tears sparkling in his eyes. "Such a moment!" he sighed, pressing a hand to his thick chest. "I have dreamed about this since my youth. To hold in my hands the *evidence* that he lived. I know it is hard for you to appreciate what this means to me. It is as if I were a Crusader about to touch the Holy Grail."

"Don't get your hopes up," I warned. "We don't know what's in that box yet."

"All the evidence points to success," he cried, eyes closed, voice trembling.

Slowly, he reached into the box and gingerly brought into the light a brittle sheet of paper, which he studied intensely before handing it to me. "Yes. These are his files," he sighed. The paper was a letter on the stationery of the President of the Board of Police Commissioners. The signature was that of Theodore Roosevelt. It bore an 1895 date. But it had nothing to do with anyone named Holmes.

The box of documents which we examined was the first of dozens, each scrutinised as excitedly by Wiggy as if it were the first rather than simply another among dozens. The search stretched into hours, then days, but though my expectations flagged early, Wiggy pressed on, working tirelessly to prove his conviction that at any moment we would come upon the answer to *the* question.

The climactic moment came late in the sixth afternoon of our search. "We have found it," stated Wiggins softly, a scrap of paper fluttering in his trembling hands.

"What is it?" I asked, awed.

"A cablegram," said Wiggy, carefully handing the yellowed paper to me. "Note the date. July 1894. At that time, Roosevelt was serving on the United States Civil Service Commission. Note that that is how the cable is addressed. Note the message *and* the signature."

The cable was brief:

"ROOSEVELT. DO NOTHING WITH THE MATERIAL
UNTIL YOU HEAR AGAIN FROM ME. ESCOTT."

"There is no doubt that we are on to something," cried my friend, poking into the papers at the bottom of the carton that had yielded the cable. "And what we are about to find is surely as delicate a matter as Holmes ever encountered, else why the necessity to continue the use of the stage name? Why the guarded reference to 'material'?"

As ever, Wiggy's deductions were telling. The cable clearly proved, he explained, that Holmes (Escott) and Roosevelt had shared an extremely sensitive experience, one so sensitive that Roosevelt had filed this cable with material from his days with the police rather than include it in his documents from his federal service. Its inclusion in these files, Wiggy reasoned, linked the cable to a police matter.

The deduction gained considerable credence with the discovery of the following letter dated in early July 1894:

Mr Sherlock Holmes

221B Baker Street

London, England

Dear Mr Holmes:

My friend Dr Watson will, I am sure, share with you my letter of this date to him complimenting him on the publication in The Strand Magazine *of his excellent stories. I eagerly await the next number in this exciting series of adventures based on your famous cases. Watson will undoubtedly inquire about the suggestion which I have made in my letter to him, namely, that he might want to look at the notes and observations which I made at the time of our very thrilling association in the matter of the Gramercy Park murder. I have gone so far as to suggest a title: "The Adventure of the Stalwart Companions." I will, of course, be guided by your wishes and look forward to receiving your views and some information on how you are and what you are up to.*

Very truly yours,

T. R.

Rubbing his hands and chuckling, Wiggy remarked, "One can imagine the haste with which Holmes shot off that cable to Teddy, eh?"

"Is there no copy of Roosevelt's letter to Watson?" I asked eagerly, kneeling on the cold floor of the basement storehouse as Wiggy picked through more bundles of papers in a deeply stuffed box.

"Nothing. I fear that one is lost. I hope there are others. And, God, I pray that Roosevelt's 'notes and observations' are to be found in these endless archives!"

Presently, Wiggy exploded with excitement, shooting upright and coming very close to performing a jig. "Eureka! The find of the century! There has never been anything like this! Look! Look, my beloved friend; a letter from *him* in his *own hand!*"

The text of the letter:

My Dear Roosevelt:

Under no circumstances must the details of the singular affair of Gramercy Park be published so long as the participants live and so long as there might be the slightest chance of repercussions.

Watson, who has written to you on this matter, will explain my reasons for insisting that certain of my cases be withheld from the public, and he will tell you, I am sure, of the numerous instances in which I have insisted that certain names, dates, locations, and some significant details of my cases be deleted or masked in the adventures he has already publicised.

It is safe to say that only a handful of my numerous investigations match the Gramercy Park affair in sinister implications and tragic aftermath.

As to the title you suggested, I can only say that I am disappointed to know that you have seen fit to indulge in the same kind of sensationalism which marks the writings of my dear friend Watson. One day I would like to read your notes on the adventure we shared, hoping to find you have not committed Watson's crime of slurring over work of the utmost finesse and delicacy in order to dwell upon sensational details which would excite but could not possibly instruct the reader.

Your servant,

S. H.

I had barely finished reading the letter, penned in the exquisitely fine hand of − I was *convinced* now − Sherlock Holmes, when Wiggy exploded again.

"Here it is! Watson's letter. The one Holmes refers to!"

The hand was bold, assured − the hand of both a doctor and an author:

Dear Mr Roosevelt:

I thank you for your very generous comments on my literary efforts recounting Holmes's work in the adventures in The Strand Magazine. *I assure you the current adventure has a most thrilling ending, but I obey your admonition not to reveal it to you in advance as I understand your desire to follow the tale in subsequent issues; which I am delighted to know you receive in America.*

Holmes has surely expressed to you personally his strong feelings on the suggestion that the adventure you and he shared be published. I know some of the facts in that serious matter and agree with my colleague that it ought to be withheld for years to come, possibly forever.

Holmes is quite set in his mind on withholding certain of the cases which he has investigated and brought to satisfactory conclusions. In a vault in the bank of Cox & Co., I keep a tin dispatch box crammed with papers, nearly all of which are records of cases to illustrate the curious problems which Holmes had at various times to examine. The discretion and high sense of professional honour which have always distinguished my friend are at work in the choice of the memoirs.

When we chance to meet again I expect to hear from you in person some of the details of the affair which you intriguingly title "The Adventure of the Stalwart Companions."'

Very truly yours,

John H. Watson, M. D.

In a matter of a few minutes, dusty and forgotten cartons in the depths of an official building in Manhattan had yielded up to my friend and me the incontrovertible evidence that Holmes and Watson had not been mere fiction from the pen of Sir Arthur Conan Doyle! Yet this astounding discovery was eclipsed by the fear Wiggy and I shared that we might not uncover the document which Holmes and Watson – and, obviously, Roosevelt – agreed could not be published in their lifetimes.

A few minutes after we uncovered Watson's letter, we found – sealed in a thick envelope – the amazing document which Roosevelt chose to call:

"The Adventure of the Stalwart Companions"

One

&

It was the last day of June 1880 when I left Harvard with my head filled with the anticipation of a thrilling journey into the plains, hills, and valleys of Iowa and Minnesota in the company of my brother, Elliott. A vacation was exactly what I needed, having just completed arduous scholarly pursuits at college. I relished the thought of spending time in the great out-of-doors, especially because I was planning further scholarship in the study of law at Columbia. I was also, at this time, on the verge of marriage, a prospect which delighted me, although my photograph taken in my senior year at Harvard by J. Notman of Boston indicates that I was a very serious-minded young man -- jaw firmly and determinedly set, the eyes unflinching, the straight nose, all bespeaking a youth of purpose. Yet the sideburns, coming very near to being muttonchop whiskers, indicate the real Roosevelt behind that sombre visage. Not rakish, precisely, but adventuresome, beyond question.

I had thoroughly enjoyed Harvard, which I had entered in the fall of 1876, and I was confident that it did me good. I had earned a Phi Beta Kappa key. I had spent a good deal of my time in studying scientific matters because when I entered college I was devoted to out-of-doors natural history. My ambition at the time was to be a scientific man of the Audubon, or Wilson, or Baird, or Coues type. Much of this interest had been tolerated in me by my father, who had told me I would have to make my own way in the world and if that meant a scientific career, I could do so. Before he died, he impressed upon me the need to be serious about my intentions. He warned that the comfortable financial situation in which he left me should not be an excuse for me to approach scientific matters as a dilettante. He also told me that if I was not going to earn money, I should even things up by not spending it. Unfortunately, Harvard disappointed me in my aims. The outdoor naturalist and observer of nature was ignored in the curriculum and biology was treated as purely a science of the laboratory and the microscope. While I was quite disappointed, I was also resolved to pursue my interests on my own, if necessary. As a result, I spent a good deal of time teaching myself by whatever means I could find. It proved difficult and I began to resign myself to giving up science as a career.

While my own scientific explorations were to leave me disappointed in terms of my own career, they were to bring me into contact with a young man residing in London, England, to whom science was also a passion and for whom the structured formalities of university science had also proved a disappointment. How I came to know this remarkable fellow is important because of subsequent events shared by the two of us, so I will devote some time here to relating how it came to pass that there had developed by the middle of the year 1880 a friendship, albeit by correspondence, between myself, Theodore Roosevelt, and Mr Sherlock Holmes.

That I should undertake a friendship through the post was not unusual for me. The writing of letters had been one of the most important contacts with the outside world in my boyhood. I had the misfortune to be a weak and sickly child. I suffered terribly from asthma and often had to be taken away on trips to find a place where I could breathe. One of my memories is of my father walking up and down the room with me in his arms at night when I was a very small person, and of sitting up in bed gasping, with my father and mother trying to help me. I went very little to school, and never to public schools because of my illnesses. I studied under tutors in the grand old house wherein I had been born on October 27, 1858, at 28 East Twentieth Street in Manhattan. It was during my childhood in that house that I developed both my interest in natural history and my penchant for keeping diaries and writing letters. I did not consider it unusual to write to strangers, such as the authors of books I had read, or to interesting personalities I encountered in newspapers or magazines.

As a habitual writer of unsolicited letters to persons I found fascinating, I quite naturally decided to write a letter to the author of a very interesting monograph which I came across in my independent readings in the library at Harvard. The work was titled: *Upon the Distinction Between the Ashes of the Various Tobaccos: An Enumeration of 140 Forms of Cigar, Cigarette and Pipe Tobacco, with Coloured Plates Illustrating the Difference in the Ash*. Its author was listed as Mr Sherlock Holmes. The address of the publisher was in London, England, and it was to that address that I sent a brief note expressing my admiration for the author's science. The response from Mr Holmes was astounding in that its author presumed on the basis of my very brief note to provide an amazingly accurate biographical sketch of myself.

"My studies of science," wrote Mr Holmes, "have gone into areas that have never been fully realised, especially in the realm of deducing facts by observation. For example, I know from your letter that you have had considerable trouble with your eyes in the past, that you are an outdoorsman, your father has some wealth, that he has been very indulgent of your rebelliousness in terms of choosing a life's work, and that at the time you wrote to me you were seated with the late afternoon sun to your back and that you were wearing a blue jacket and were penning your letter at the university library." Anticipating my amazement, Holmes went on to explain these startling statements. "Your eye trouble is evident in the very careful penmanship which is produced by someone who has learned to write by bending very close to the paper – a habit developed at a time of troubled vision which has, I assume, been corrected, though the habit of bending over so far persists along with the careful writing. The business of being an outdoorsman I deduce from both your stated interest in natural science and the fact that your penmanship is hurried, indicating restlessness at being cooped up in a room. That your family has some wealth is obvious enough, inasmuch as you are a student at Harvard, which I know to be an institution of some distinction and some cost to its students. Because you are a native New Yorker, you would have chosen a school closer to home if expenses had been a problem. I surmise that your father's wealth comes from business interests which you do not share, given your stated interest in natural science; ergo, your father must be a very tolerant man to permit you to pursue science when he would probably prefer you to follow him in his business. That you chose not to indicates rebelliousness. As for your blue suit, a strand of fiber was adhered to the writing paper. On the location of the sun to your back and that it was a late afternoon sun, I make these deductions on the basis of a slight blotting of the paper by your hand, unnoticed because of a waning light as you wrote. That you did your penmanship in the library I deduce from the fact that the nib of your pen was quite worn—the type found in library ink stands – and that you wrote regarding my monograph on tobaccos which you had read at the library in question. All quite elementary, you see."

It may seem superfluous to state that I could not resist continuing to correspond with a young man of such unusual and amazing talents. In my next letter to him I went on at some length in praise of his abilities, to which he responded, "The science of deduction and analysis is one which can only be acquired by long and patient study, yet, from a drop of water a logician could infer the possibility of an Atlantic or a Niagara without having seen or heard of one or the other. All of life is a great chain, the nature of which is known whenever we are shown a single link of it. By a man's fingernails, by his coat-sleeve, by his boots, by his trouser-knees, by the callosities of his forefinger and thumb, by his expression, by his shirt-cuffs – by each of these things a man's calling is plainly revealed. That all united should fail to enlighten the competent inquirer in any case is almost inconceivable. To illustrate some of this, I am taking the liberty of sending you further writings on the study of footprints and the dating of documents. If you are interested, I have other writings which I would be happy to send to you. In your latest letter you seem to have implied that my deductions in your case were little more than a clever trick, but I assure you, Mr Roosevelt, that I am in earnest. In fact, I am beginning to earn my living with these skills as a consulting detective. I believe I am the only one in the world."

Thus began a regular exchange of letters between myself at Harvard and Mr Holmes, who was residing in lodgings on Montague Street in London. The letters revealed a remarkable mind and a great talent for the career which he had chosen to pursue. They also revealed a man of surprises, the greatest of which was his announcement that he had undertaken the study of acting, theatrical makeup, and costuming because, as he put it, "I have need of these skills in my work." He wrote of a decision to go on the stage for a time as a member of a troupe of Shakespearean players under Mr Michael Sasanoff. "I have quite a flair for this acting business," he wrote. Subsequently, he added that the

Sasanoff troupe would be touring America and that he would be appearing in New York beginning in January 1880. "I trust you will come to see me," he said. Still later, in a note from a hotel in Union Square, Manhattan, he wrote, "Your latest letter indicates you will pass through New York on your way West after your graduation. I hope you will come to see my Malvolio in *Twelfth Night*. I am arranging for a pair of tickets for you for the evening performance, Friday, July 2. By the way, my stage name is William Escott, a private joke which I will explain when, at last, we meet. Holmes."

An evening at the theatre was something that I infrequently appreciated, but I looked forward to the production of *Twelfth Night* with the anticipation of seeing Mr Holmes as a performer prior to meeting him, at last, in person. My eagerness was increased when I decided to make a test of Mr Holmes's abilities as a detective by the device of inviting a young acquaintance of mine to attend the theatre with me.

I chose as my companion Mr Wilson Hargreave, himself a detective with the New York Police Department.

Just as I gave Holmes no clue that my companion would be a detective, neither did I let Hargreave know the real identity or the real profession of the man we were to greet backstage.

It would be, I expected, a delightful evening of discovery for all.

Two

Detective Wilson Hargreave was an exception among the men of the New York Police Department, which was caught up in one of the worst scandals of its existence, the awful allegations of corruption, brutality, and malfeasance reaching to the highest echelons of Mulberry Street. I do not allege that every member of the police force was corrupt, but the malaise was widespread and the daily newspapers were filled with the scandal, the notoriety of which was having its effect on the good and honest men of the force who were simply trying to do their jobs. This was the situation facing Will Hargreave, and I assumed it was the severity of the strain which was evident upon his face as I welcomed him to the Roosevelt house on Fifty-seventh Street, just around the corner from Fifth Avenue.

Though his handsome features were clouded by all the conditions which I have described, he made an effort to be cheerful. "Good evening, Teddy," he smiled, taking my hand firmly as I opened the door. "It's good to have you back in New York."

"It's good to see you, Will," I said, clapping him on the shoulder.

"Come in. We have a few minutes to renew our friendship before we head downtown to the theatre."

Will Hargreave and I had known each other since adolescence, though our first meeting had found us on less than friendly terms. I came to know him because his father had begun a business relationship with my father. The boy had come with his father on an occasion to our house on Twentieth Street. He evinced what appeared to be a dislike of me based solely on my physical appearance. "You wear eyeglasses," he noted.

"I do," I replied firmly, studying him through my thick lenses and noting the strong resemblance to his father – a youth of English stock, slender but sturdy, a straight nose, slightly cleft chin, firm mouth, unflinching grey-green eyes. He was my age but slightly taller and considerably more muscular. "Have you never seen anyone who wears eyeglasses?" I inquired.

"Of course I have. Girls and sissies," he chuckled.

Could he, I wondered, with regret, be a bully-boy of the type I had known in school? If so, I surmised, I would have to set him straight. "While our fathers are conducting their business," I suggested, "perhaps you would like to see something of my favourite hobby?"

"Hobby?" he smirked. "What would it be? Butterflies? A rock collection?"

"Come along and you will see," I said, beckoning him to follow me to the second-floor porch which my father had outfitted as a gymnasium. Promptly I found two pairs of boxing mitts. The gymnasium was fully equipped. It was as complete as any in the city for me to use in building up my physique after those childhood illnesses. "You do box?" I asked, pushing a pair of mitts toward him.

"I do," he grinned, "and very well, I warn you."

Pulling on my gloves, I replied, "Bully!"

Having removed his jacket, he concerned himself with donning his gloves while watching me amusedly. "Ought you not remove your eyeglasses?" he asked.

"No need. You shan't lay a glove upon me."

He laughed at this and came toward me, a rather poor example of the proper way for a youth to posture himself when wearing boxing mitts. Confidently, I permitted him the first blow, which I parried easily, leaving him open to my rather wicked right. I felt his nose give under my blow, and he went down immediately, bleeding from the nostrils. His spirit was not broken, but when I refused to continue, however, he did not insist that we go on. "I'll make no more wiseacre remarks about your glasses," he announced.

"Excellent," I said, helping him to his feet.

"You really meant business," he smiled.

"Certainly. I take very seriously some advice my father gave me concerning fisticuffs. He has always advised not to get into a fight if you can possibly avoid it. If you do get in, see it through. But never hit soft, and if you must hit a man, *put him to sleep.*"

"You have a wise father."

"Yes, I do, thanks be to God."

I never had cause to hit Hargreave again because we became fast friends.

"Harvard has had an effect upon you, Teddy."

"In what way? I'm the same as I was before I went to Massachusetts."

"I refer to your rather surprising invitation to attend the theatre. I never knew you were a playgoing sort."

"An apt observation. Plays make me fidgety, but—"

"Something about this play is unique."

"I would venture to say that Shakespeare is always unique."

"You know what I'm getting at," Hargreave smiled.

"No, I don't, Will."

"Of all the friends you have in New York society, friends who would welcome an evening with Shakespeare, you called upon me to accompany you. I have accepted because I am intrigued to know why."

"Oh, Will, you cut me to the quick. It's your companionship I sought. I have no ulterior motives."

"Teddy, your whole life has been built upon ulterior motives."

"And you, Will, have the soul of a policeman. Do you ever accept anything for what it seems on the surface?"

"That, to a policeman, would be a perilous flaw."

"I assure you, Will, I have in mind only an evening at the theater and, afterward, supper with a fellow by the name of William Escott."

"A classmate?"

"In fact, Mr Escott is one of the actors in the play we shall see."

"So, your interest in the theatre goes beyond merely attending plays. You have now taken up the company of players. Shall we be off, then?"

"Ah, a cab right outside the door," I said as we ventured onto the rainy stoop.

"I've booked it for the night, given the inclement weather," said Hargreave, opening the door for me.

"But why a four-wheeler?" I asked, settling comfortably in the carriage as Hargreave climbed in, sitting opposite me.

"Merely to avoid being cramped into one of those infamous small hacks," he grinned. "Lucky for us that I booked a larger one inasmuch as we are going to be joined by this actor-friend of yours."

We set off at a good pace down Fifth Avenue, snug against the wet and unusual chill for the second day of July. Before long, Hargreave was peeking at his timepiece. "You are quite concerned with the time," I remarked.

"He's due at the ferry slip at this hour."

"Who is due at the ferry slip?"

"President Hayes."

"The President? I had no idea the Chief Executive was in the city."

"It's a private visit. He is dining with the German Consul General on a vessel of the North German Lloyds Steamship Company at their pier in Hoboken. He goes over by ferry at about this time."

"Are you concerned for his safety?"

"The New York Police Department is always concerned about the safety of the Chief Executive when he is in the city."

"But you seem especially concerned."

"I don't mean to give that impression. It's just that I am on call. Not only in the case of the President, but for anything unusual that may occur."

"Has it anything to do with the recent rumour concerning the President?"

"You heard about that rumour even at Harvard?"

"It was in the newspapers that a story had gone around that Mr. Hayes had died mysteriously. That was a few weeks ago."

"It was a rumour, nothing more."

"The reports were vague about the possible source of that scurrilous tale," I noted.

"There were other reports that were suppressed from the newspapers," said the young detective gravely.

"Those rumours account for the extra concern by the police about Mr Hayes' visit?"

"Yes."

"Is he in danger?"

"No."

"You'll rest more easily when he has departed the city."

"A policeman always rests more easily when his beat has returned to its accustomed routines. A policeman on patrol is happiest when he has nothing untoward to report at the end of his duty. A detective has his most successful day when he does not have to venture from the station house on a case."

"I suspect the worst your police officers will have to handle is a few citizens who imbibe a bit too much in celebration of the Fourth of July."

"You have more faith in the common man than I, but you are not a policeman."

"It is not the common man who does the most damage to a society, Will. A man of great wealth who does not use that wealth decently is a menace to the community. I do not fear the common man. I fear the man with enough money to afford to finance corruption."

"That sounds like a political speech. Are you running for something?"

"Perhaps I will, one day."

"Excellent, Teddy. I'll vote for you."

Three

I had always enjoyed returning to New York City, and on this occasion, marking yet another celebration of the birth of our nation, the residents seemed determined to enjoy themselves as never before. They were, perhaps, encouraged in their private celebrations by the peculiar lack of an official demonstration for Independence Day – there being no parade.

As we proceeded toward Union Square, I was somewhat unpleasantly surprised to find that the 'Rialto' section of theatres, eating establishments, and other types of commerce connected with nightlife was marching steadily northward from its customary environs so that all of Broadway between Union Square and Forty-second Street was awash with New Yorkers seeking the pleasures of an often boisterous nightlife.

Coming into Union Square, our carriage slowed in order not to run over pedestrians who showed a decided lack of concern for themselves and others by dashing in a most dangerous way into the streets in their fever for divertissements. Union Square was as garish as ever, except for the staid presence of Tiffany's and Brentano's, those conservative establishments appearing not at all embarrassed by the brashness of the city's theatrical district, even in its off season. Directly ahead of us on the south side of a pleasant park of greenery and public monuments that stood amidst a swirl of commerce loomed the Union Square Theatre, its billboards proudly announcing the performances of the heralded Sasanoff troupe.

In the misty distance, the towers of the Brooklyn Bridge, still under construction after so many years of labour, rose above the rooftops of the lower east side of Manhattan. I remarked upon the impressive evidence of this new link between Manhattan and Brooklyn to Hargreave, who responded with a nod. He had been lost in thought during the entire journey downtown and was barely more interested in the recognising greeting – a salute – offered by a member of the police department's Broadway Squad, a team of especially fine-looking men whose gentlemanly appearances masked well-trained physiques especially suited for handling any of the untoward occurrences that might come about in an area of the city vulnerable to thieves, pickpockets, and other thugs who might choose to prey upon happy theatregoers.

"If you are not in the mood for the theatre," I remarked as we stepped from our carriage, "I will be most understanding."

With a quick, reassuring smile, Hargreave touched my sleeve and replied, "I'm sorry, Teddy. I have been very inhospitable."

"You have the President's welfare on your mind."

"This being an election year, feelings are running high," he said, "but I promise you that I will now put that from my mind and concentrate on Mr Shakespeare's *Twelfth Night*."

The Sasanoff players had attracted a full house and our host – Mr Escott/Holmes – had provided us with choice seats close to the stage and in the centre. A few moments after we had made ourselves comfortable, the lights dimmed and the curtain rose.

The role of Malvolio is a minor one, so I am certain that Hargreave and I were the only members of the audience who awaited with any expectancy the appearance of the character.

There entered in the fifth scene a lean, almost gangling youth with a remarkable stage presence for one so tender in years. It was evident that something in the way the young actor moved, something in his eyes, something in his young but commanding style attracted all eyes in the audience to him as the character Olivia turned to Malvolio to ask, "How say you to that, Malvolio?"

"I marvel your ladyship takes delight in such a barren rascal," he replied.

The voice was light and airy, befitting the character of Olivia's steward. When he spoke his next line I found myself wondering if the young actor were describing himself, although speaking the line as Shakespeare wrote it: "Not yet old enough for a man, nor young enough for a boy."

In a whisper, Hargreave remarked, "This friend of yours is quite good."

I was not accustomed to being behind the scenes at a theatre and was impressed by the machinery of the stage – the ropes, pulleys, weights, and other paraphernalia by which curtains were raised, scenery shifted and the general fantasy world of theatrics produced. An usher to whom I had given my card to be taken backstage to Mr Escott had returned to announce that Mr Escott was delightedly waiting to greet me and my companion in his dressing room. "Be careful of the stairs going down," warned the usher.

The dressing room was located well below the level of the theatre's auditorium in what, if the theatre had been a ship, would have been steerage. Locating a door that promised to open into Mr Sherlock Holmes' dressing room – a slip of paper tacked to the wooden door bore the inscription "Escott," I rapped sharply upon it and was answered by a brusque voice. "Who is it?"

"Roosevelt," I announced through the door.

"The door is open. Come in. Mind the clutter."

Seated with his back toward us was Escott — that is, Holmes — a lean young man with a narrow face that was dominated by a hawklike nose and a pointed chin. His complexion appeared ruddy, but this proved to be an illusion caused by the vigorous rubbing of the skin with great gobs of cleansing cream applied with swabs of cotton as the young actor proceeded to remove the makeup that had changed that face to Malvolio's.

"Good evening, Holmes," I said as we entered.

"Ah, Mr Roosevelt!" he exclaimed as he saw me reflected in his mirror. Rising to greet us, he was impressively tall but shockingly thin. "I aim delighted that you came. How did you like the play?" he asked, enthusiastically shaking my hand. "And who is this?" he inquired, turning to Hargreave.

"Permit me to introduce my companion for the evening, Mr Wilson Hargreave. Will, this is—"

"Mr William Escott, I was led to believe?"

Holmes bowed. "My stage name. I am Sherlock Holmes. William Escott is a play upon my given names."

"A clever alias, sir. I compliment you on it and your performance," said Hargreave.

"Please be seated, gentlemen. I do not have a very large dressing room, but we shan't be long. I need only a moment more to remove this makeup."

"Don't rush on our behalf," I said cheerily.

"The art of makeup and disguise fascinates me," said Holmes, turning again to study himself in the mirror. "I have played much older men through proper makeup and I have seen very old actors become youths with a bit of putty and a dash of color."

"Your Malvolio was a revelation," I replied.

"Thank you," said Holmes, showing a fleeting smile in the mirror. Then his eyes turned to Hargreave and he stated, "You are quite a young man to be a member of the ranks of the detectives of the New York Police Department, Hargreave."

"Holmes, you amaze me!" I gasped.

"Do I indeed?" he laughed. "Do I amaze you, Mr Hargreave?"

"I must confess that you do."

"Nothing amazing about it, really," Holmes shrugged. Turning back to his mirror, he dabbed at the last smudges of theatrical makeup. "Elementary deduction. I am disappointed in you, Roosevelt, however. I had thought you would have expected me to see immediately that your companion at the theatre tonight is a member of the constabulary in your fascinating city."

"Mr Holmes has made a science of deduction," I ventured to explain to Hargreave.

"Not a science, more of an art at this point," insisted Holmes. "Do you know much about the art of deduction, Mr Hargreave?"

"Can't say that I do."

"There is an article of some interest on it, in the *Harper's* magazine of June. It is a review of a new book by one Noah K. Davis titled "The Theory of Thought, A Treatise on Deductive Logic." I am intrigued by the article and am looking forward to obtaining the book. I shall send you a copy."

"Mr Holmes uses the sci– uh, the *art*, of deduction in his practice. He is a consulting detective in London," I explained.

"You are a detective?" asked Hargreave.

"I am not connected with any official police agency. I am a private consulting detective."

"Fascinating, sir."

"The more so because I have determined to use and to perfect as much as possible the detective's greatest tool in the solving of crimes, his powers of deductive reasoning and objective observation."

"By which methods you deduced that I am a detective?"

"Precisely."

"Forgive me, but I find it more reasonable to assume that you had read my name in newspaper accounts."

"By Jove, I have!" laughed Holmes.

"So you knew from the newspapers that Will is a detective," I interjected, obviously showing my disappointment.

"Yes, I have read your name in the news columns, but I recalled this only because you suggested it as an explanation for my knowing your occupation. I am acutely embarrassed that I did not make the connection between the Mr Hargreave standing here in my cramped dressing room and the W. Hargreave of the newspapers. I deduced your connection with the police solely by observing and listening during the first few moments when we met."

"Am I that obvious?"

"Not to the untrained observer. To an ordinary criminal you would give no clues that you possess a policeman's badge. You do possess one! It makes an almost imperceptible bulge in the line of your jacket, kept in a wallet in your inside breast pocket on your left side. Hardly more noticeable is the slight deviation in the line of your jacket at your right hip where you carry your revolver."

"I shall speak to my tailor," said Hargreave, patting his hip. "I have coats especially cut to make allowances for the weapon. He has obviously not done a very good job of it."

"On the contrary, my compliments to him. Only a trained eye would notice it and the other bulge in your pocket where, I believe, you keep a set of those interesting devices called handcuffs which you Americans have recently improved upon."

"Self-locking ones," nodded Hargreave. "They snap shut immediately when placed on the wrists, thus allowing a policeman to apply the cuffs with one hand while holding on to his suspect with the other."

"But you gave me one other clue that led me to make a very cursory examination of your appearance to see if my impression that you are a policeman would hold up."

"Another clue?"

"I told you Escott was my stage name; you called it an alias."

"Very astute, sir."

"Astute observation and deductive reasoning will reveal the truth in any situation as surely as cold cream has revealed my true face beneath the actor's mask. Now that I am a respectable member of society, I suggest some supper. I have numerous questions to ask Hargreave about the techniques of the New York Police Department, and Roosevelt, I am in your debt for your delightful decision to bring Hargreave along."

"May I suggest supper at the Hoffman House?" I said.

"An excellent and famous cuisine," nodded Hargreave.

"Yes," winked Holmes, "and an establishment that is equally famous for its Bouguereau's nude surrounded by satyrs that hangs above the bar."

"You've come to know a good deal about New York, Mr Holmes," observed Hargreave.

"It is a city second only to London in its potential for criminal activity. Shall we go?"

Delighted at seeing the two detectives taking so readily to one another, I followed them through the drafty wings of the theatre, out the stage door and into the rainy night.

"What about Roosevelt? Has he the makings of a detective?" asked Holmes, clapping me on the shoulder.

"I can't say," chuckled Hargreave, "but if you ever need a man to do some fighting — fisticuffs — Teddy's your man."

"Is that so, Roosevelt? You seem such a quiet fellow."

"Teddy speaks quietly but carries a big fist," laughed Hargreave. "Believe me, I know."

In this light and playful mood, we headed up Broadway to Madison Square and the Hoffman House with its nude and satyrs and deliciously appointed bill of fare.

Four

I have not had such marvellous company at a meal," announced Sherlock Holmes, dabbing his mouth with a napkin, "since breakfast at Delmonico's a fortnight ago. It was a farewell for Mr Edwin Booth, prior to his leaving for Europe. I had the improbable pleasure of sitting between Mr P. T. Barnum and Chief Justice Shea."

"I have thoroughly enjoyed myself, Mr Holmes," said Hargreave, leaning back and contentedly puffing on a cigar.

"I note from the fragrance of your smoke that you accept the new fashion of wrapping cigars in Sumatran leaf, rather than the Cuban which has heretofore been so popular in the States," said Holmes. Choosing for his after-dinner smoke a curved briar which he deftly packed with a dark shag, he continued to speak between the puffs as he put a match to his bowl. He became a picture of alternately flaring flame and billowing clouds of smoke. "The Sumatra wrapper gives a thin and silky flavour, of course," he added. "I know quite a bit about tobacco and have written a monograph on the subject as it relates to criminal investigations. A man's cigar ash is as peculiar a signature as the shape of his ear or the imprinted pattern of his fingertips, but for real individuality in smoking I give you the pipe. Nothing has more individuality, except, perhaps, watches and bootlaces. For example, you have shown a considerable interest through the evening in your own timepiece, Hargreave."

"Have I?"

"Now, you know you have, Will," I chuckled.

"I have not peeked at my watch at all during this dinner," my friend objected, drawing the handsome timepiece from his waistcoat pocket.

"But you made several references to it during *Twelfth Night*," asserted Holmes with a satisfied puff on his briar.

"Well," shrugged Hargreave, "apparently actors in a play watch the audience even as the audience watches them."

"It was my curiosity to know if Roosevelt had accepted my invitation to the play which drew my attention to the pair of seats I had reserved for him," explained Holmes, "but when I peered over the footlights to the location of your seats and found you, Hargreave, constantly looking at your watch, I began to wonder if our performance was really that tedious."

With a laugh, I explained, "Will is on call this evening and is a bit on edge, especially in view of the President's visit to our city."

"I see," nodded Holmes. "Is there reason for concern about Mr Hayes?"

"No," said Hargreave, reassuringly shaking his head and replacing his watch in his pocket. "He's dining as a guest of the German Consul General aboard a German steamship."

"And you had been keeping an eye on your watch as a means of knowing how much longer it would be until the President leaves the ship for his hotel rather than as an expression of displeasure at my performance."

"Exactly, though I am amused that you bothered to worry about me and my watch instead of your lines while you were performing on stage."

"The stage is a marvellous podium from which to observe mankind."

"Your clients must be constantly startled by you and your methods," I interjected.

"I have no interest in my clients except as they are factors in a problem. Emotion is antagonistic to reasoning. I do not consider personalities in my decisions as to which problems to undertake. I generally choose to be associated with those crimes which present some difficulty in their solution. These are usually the simpler crimes. It is in unimportant matters that one finds a field for observation, for the quick analysis of cause and effect which gives charm to an investigation. The larger the crime the more obvious the motive. Give me the commonplace, for it is there where one finds the most intricate puzzles. I recently had a problem concerning one of this city's first families. A rifled safe. A common prime. But it was the fact that the glass of the conservatory door must have been broken from the inside that led me to the family footman as the culprit."

"I was not aware of a crime affecting one of our notable families," frowned Hargreave.

Holmes shrugged. "The family called upon me because they did not want any publicity, you see. As for you, Hargreave, duty is about to take you from us! A very imposing fellow in a policeman's uniform is making his way as rapidly as possible across this room in our direction. I expect you are about to be summoned to an investigation."

The tall, burly, red-haired policeman apologised for disturbing us, then announced, "There has been a murder, Mr Hargreave."

"Where?" asked the detective.

"At Gramercy Park, sir."

"Well, it's a fashionable murder," asserted Holmes.

Hargreave flashed a smile. "You do know our city, Mr Holmes."

"I am familiar with Gramercy Park merely because I chance to have rooms at number 39 East Twenty-second Street, which is a short walk from Gramercy Park."

"I am sorry about being called away like this," said Hargreave, rising from his chair and carefully placing his napkin on the tablecloth.

"We'll have dinner again," I announced emphatically.

"Hargreave," said Holmes softly, "I am not certain of the protocol, if there might be a violation of regulations but—"

Hargreave gave a quick, delighted laugh. "Of course! Come along. You, too, Teddy."

"What?" I gasped.

"This will not take very long, I'm sure," said Hargreave. "Then we can resume our conversation elsewhere."

"That's a bully idea," I said, thumping a hand on the table.

"I'm sure this is a routine, common street crime," Hargreave continued.

"Ah, but there is nothing as uncommon as a common crime, Hargreave," stated Holmes, his narrowed eyes flashing cold as steel. "Shall we be off then?"

"Yes, indeed," said Hargreave.

"Come on, Teddy," said Holmes enthusiastically. "The game's afoot."

The distance from the Hoffman House to Gramercy Park was not a long one, and our four-wheeler had us there in quick time. A fog shrouded the dark and nearly deserted streets. Wet pavements reflected flickering gaslamps while the same lights made darkly grotesque shapes of the trees in a small square park bounded on four sides by the elegant houses of Gramercy Park, the last neighborhood in the city where one would expect a murder to be done.

On the way as we passed from Broadway onto Twentieth Street, I pointed out to Holmes the address where I had spent most of my childhood – the house where, on the second storey, I had floored Hargreave with one punch. Holmes' response to this fascinating moment of personal history was a mere grunt, but not so much as a glance out the window of the four-wheeler. Holmes leaned forward, his arm propped on a bony knee, his pointy chin resting on his fist, lost in thought.

The carriage drew to a stop before number 15 and Holmes followed Hargreave out of the cab, bounding to the sidewalk where, beneath a policeman's raincoat, sprawled the corpse. Holmes removed the covering and studied the body of the hapless victim, back and front. Replacing the raincoat, Holmes rose and strode away a few steps, paused by a lamppost, then returned and studied the dead man again. "Odd," he muttered, rising again.

"What do you make of it, Mr Holmes?" asked Hargreave, who had studied the body himself.

"I should like to know if the police have an official explanation for what has happened here."

"Of course," said Hargreave, signalling to one of the uniformed officers. "Sergeant, what is the official surmise regarding this incident?"

The police sergeant eyed Holmes with curiosity, then proceeded to relate what had occurred. "The man was shot in the back. Robbery attempt, we believe. His name is Nigel Tebbel. We know this from papers in his wallet."

"I see," said Holmes. "Witnesses?"

"The neighbours," said the sergeant, waving a hand toward the surrounding houses, each aglow with light, many of whose occupants stood in doorways or porches, observing us.

"And?" said Holmes.

"And?" replied the sergeant.

"What do they testify? These neighbours?"

"They say they heard an altercation."

"An altercation? Can you be more precise?"

"Residents heard a shout and then a shot. They saw Tebbel fall to the ground."

"Curious," said Holmes. "What else?"

"It appears that Tebbel was set upon from behind by a robber. They struggled. Tebbel called for help, but there was no time for that. He was shot for his trouble."

"And fell dead here?" asked Holmes.

"Fell dead here, shot in the back by his assailant."

"By a robber?"

"By a robber," nodded the sergeant.

"His money and valuables were taken?" asked Holmes, peering across the street at the murky shadows of the trees and bushes of Gramercy Park.

"No. The robber apparently had no time. The victim's shout for help apparently scared him off."

"Time to shoot him but not enough time to rob him, eh? Curious. Thank you, Sergeant."

"A very common occurrence, Mr Holmes, Perhaps in London a street assault ending in murder is a rare thing," said Hargreave.

"Far from rare, Hargreave, but this is not a common street murder."

This assertion, uttered emphatically by Holmes, was followed by a moment of stunned silence. Hargreave, myself, and the policemen involved in the investigation ceased all activity. Every head turned to the tall, lean, angular Englishman, who paid no heed to any of us but quickly dropped to one knee to again whisk aside the rain-dampened coat which had been draped over the victim.

"Bring a lamp here, Officer," Holmes demanded, wagging a long finger at a young patrolman standing nearby. "Shine the light on the wound so Hargreave may examine it closely."

My friend Hargreave gave me a questioning look, then shrugged, and knelt on the wet pavement beside Holmes, the two detectives peering intently at the bloody hole in the back of the dead man's coat.

"Well?" demanded Holmes.

"Well what?" responded Hargreave.

"What do you make of it, man?"

"A bullet wound, of course."

"Look closely, Hargreave. For God's sake, it's plain to see if only you will look beyond the obvious."

"See what?" responded Hargreave, his voice betraying his frustration and hinting at a rising anger.

"Permit me to ask you a question, Hargreave. If I were to place the muzzle of a gun at your chest and fire a bullet into you, what would be the immediate effect of the shot?"

"To kill me, I suppose."

"That is not the immediate effect."

Hargreave frowned and studied the corpse again. "A bullet hole," he stated, softly.

"Exactly! A hole, Hargreave! And what about the bullet hole?"

"There would be traces of gunpowder."

"Precisely! I call your attention to the powder traces on this man."

Hargreave guided the hand of the patrolman holding the lantern so as to play the most possible light upon the wound in the back of the hapless Nigel Tebbel. "There are no powder traces," he pointed out to Holmes, still leaning over the man, the detectives' faces so close as to be touching.

"There you have it," crowed Holmes, rearing back in triumph. "There… are… no… powder… marks. And what does that say to you?"

Hargreave came to his feet and stared down at the body. Slowly shaking his head, he replied, "The man was not shot at close range."

"Not shot in the kind of close encounter we have heard described by persons who presume to have seen what happened here tonight."

"You mean, they are wrong?"

"They are probably wrong if their assertions are that this man was shot pointblank in a struggle with a common street robber. This unfortunate soul was shot from some distance. I would venture the opinion that he died of a bullet fired from over there. By that lamppost."

"That is half a block away, Holmes."

"Yes, and if you will examine closely a smudge on the column of that lamppost, I believe you will see exactly the kind of powder mark that would have been on this man's clothing had he died as has been described by these witnesses."

"But, how do you know…?"

"Because it was evident to me immediately that this fellow was shot at a distance and that he was running at the time he was shot."

"Really, Holmes," cried Hargreave.

"Elementary. If you assume that this man's body was subject to all the laws of physics, then the position of his body on this sidewalk indicates that he was moving away from the assailant who shot him. Look at the scuffed condition of the toes of his shoes, observe the tear in the left knee of his trousers, the lacerations on his face, indicating that he did not merely drop to the ground after being shot. He was propelled forward and onto his face. The fall tore his trousers and scuffed his shoes. The force of the shot in the back flung him to the pavement."

"Amazing."

"Not at all. When you eliminate the impossible, whatever you have left, no matter how improbable, is the truth. We know it is impossible for this man to have died in the way these witnesses testified. Therefore, he died in the only other manner possible. Namely, the one which I described. He was running. Running away from an assailant who wanted this man dead so much that he stopped, leaned against that lamppost, steadied his gun hand, aimed, and fired with deadly accuracy at a target moving rapidly away from him."

"Premeditated murder, then? Not a chance murder in the course of robbery," whispered Hargreave.

"Murder by plan. With intent," said Holmes, poking a fingertip into Hargreave's chest for punctuation.

"But why?" I interjected, stepping forward boldly.

Holmes turned his flinty eyes toward me. "Why? That, dear Roosevelt, is the question."

"But if what you say is correct, and I believe it is, how do you explain the testimony of the witnesses who said they heard a man shout for help, saw a struggle, heard a shot, and watched the murderer run away?" I asked.

"That is merely what these decent people thought they saw."

"You can explain their error?" I remarked tartly.

"It is quite simple. They heard a shout. Possibly this man calling for help. Possibly his assailant calling him to halt. That's not important. Someone shouted. The shout was followed by a shot, almost immediately. No, in fact, immediately. Frightened and startled, persons in these gracious homes cautiously drew back their curtains and peered out through wet windows, through a mist that would do London justice. They saw the shadows of trees cast by flickering gaslights. How many times, as a child on a stormy night, dear Roosevelt, did you mistake a shadow on your nursery wall for an animal or some hideous ogre straight out of a fairy tale?"

"They saw shadows?" I asked.

"And thought they saw what they subsequently described, which, we have shown, they could not have seen, because this fellow Tebbel was shot in the back while running from a gun in the hand of an unknown killer who stood beneath that lamppost and took careful aim to be sure he succeeded in his job," said Holmes. "Do you concur, Hargreave?"

"It appears that it happened as you described, Holmes."

"Then we need only discern why," I stated.

"How easy you make it seem, Roosevelt," chuckled Holmes, striding away and peering at the front of the house before which the crime had been committed. "This is an imposing house. Gramercy Park South, number 15. Whose house is this?"

"The Sage of Gramercy Park," I replied.

"The Sage of… ?" responded Holmes.

"Samuel J. Tilden lives here," Hargreave interjected.

"*The* Samuel J. Tilden?" asked Holmes.

"*The*," nodded Hargreave.

"Very curious;" Holmes nodded, "that this seemingly common murder which turns out to be uncommon has happened on the very doorstep of a man who was the unsuccessful candidate for President of the United States in the most unusual election in the history of your noble democracy."

"You amaze me with your knowledge of our country," said Hargreave.

"I cannot claim credit," Holmes replied. "I do not usually interest myself in politics, not even the politics of England and the Empire, except as politics crosses paths with crime – which is a far more common occurrence than you might imagine."

"This is New York City, Holmes," said Hargreave. "We know about the frequent correlation between crime and politics."

"It was my brother Mycroft who kept me informed of the extraordinary election involving Tilden and Hayes. Mycroft is the politically-oriented Holmes brother. The only political opinion I have ever expressed concerning the United States of America is that her separation from England in 1776 was a great mistake and that the future of the world demands an eventual reconciliation of these two great

English-speaking peoples. As to the process which was involved in the election of President Hayes and the defeat of Mr Tilden, I know only the scantiest details."

"The election was disputed and the Congress took the unusual step of establishing an elections commission to decide the outcome. The body decided in favour of all Republicans. Tilden, to his eternal credit, advised his followers to accept the verdict quietly."

"A noble gesture," nodded Holmes.

"Surely, Holmes, you are not suggesting a connection between this murder and the fact that this is Mr. Tilden's house?" asked Hargreave.

"Perhaps it is merely a coincidence," said Holmes.

"I'm sure it is," said I with a confident smile.

"Still," muttered Holmes, striding away from us in the direction from which the slain man had evidently been running, "if you were to venture an opinion as to where Tebbel was running when he was shot down, it would not be unreasonable to assume that he was heading for that door with the number 15 upon it."

Five

In the examination of the corpse, what else was found on his person in addition to the identifying papers?" inquired Holmes.

Signalling a roundsman to bring him a small sack containing the worldly possessions found on the late Mr Tebbel, Hargreave poked through the items. "Not much here. A key, a scrap of paper with the letters *C* and *G* jotted upon, it, the man's billfold which lists his name but no address, a couple of cigars – cheap ones from their aroma, and a small tin that contains a white powder which we have not yet identified."

"May I see the items?" asked Holmes.

With a nod, Hargreave handed over the miserable assortment of belongings. Holmes examined all of them in the flickering light from the lamps on the imposing facade of the Tilden house. "A hotel key," he remarked. "It has the number 405 scratched into it. Crudely done. A room number."

"Or an address," suggested Hargreave.

"Perhaps, but people usually remember their addresses. I believe it is a hotel room key. The tin of powder is cocaine."

"Cocaine?" muttered Hargreave. "As good a guess as any."

"It is cocaine. Your laboratory will confirm it," said Holmes impatiently, returning the tin of powder to Hargreave. "You see, I never guess. It is destructive to the faculty of logic," Holmes went on tartly. "May I see the man's billfold? Ah, here it is. I say, Hargreave, you didn't tell me that this fellow had a great deal of cash in his possession."

"Less than a hundred dollars," shrugged Hargreave, taking the billfold from Holmes and counting the currency inside.

"How very peculiar," observed Holmes.

"It was that amount of money which led us to assume the motive was robbery. Someone saw this Tebbel in a saloon, we surmised, saw him flash his billfold and the cash within…"

"A fair assumption on the surface, but it doesn't hold up in view of our knowledge that robbery was not the motive."

"Just a moment, sir," retorted Hargreave, growing agitated again. "I agree that Tebbel was shot from a distance, but that does not rule out robbery as the motive."

"But no money was taken. Odd behaviour for a man who has just killed in order to obtain that money," replied Holmes.

"The coming out of witnesses frightened him away," I suggested.

"A man with a gun who has committed murder for money is not going to be intimidated by unarmed and frightened citizens while he still holds the gun in his hand, a smoking gun at that," Holmes said, striding back to the corpse once more. "I am fascinated by the presence of so much money on this fellow's person when, if you will look at his shoes, notice the rundown heels, the small hole where the sole of his left shoe has been worn through."

The man's shoes were as Holmes described – quite worn down.

"A poor suit of clothes, as well," I noted.

"Excellent, Roosevelt. A shabby suit, indeed! Hardly the attire of a man who goes about with one hundred dollars in his purse. We now have three perplexing questions before us: Who shot this man, why, and what circumstances led to this unlikely fellow having so much money in his pocket-book?"

"And has your deductive power answered those questions?" asked Hargreave irritably.

Holmes shrugged, "If so, you, Hargreave, would be on your way to an arrest in this case. I do not, unfortunately, have the answers to our three questions, but this is an interesting problem, and we do have something to go on. A key, a scrap of paper with two letters jotted on it, and the incontrovertible fact that Nigel Tebbel was shot to death from a motive far more sinister and intricate than mere murder for profit. Would you object, Hargreave, if I were to work on this very interesting problem?"

"It will be interesting for me to observe your methods," said Hargreave.

"They may prove somewhat unusual," replied Holmes.

"You will, of course, keep me informed?"

"From moment to moment."

"May I ask how you plan to begin your investigation?"

"By learning precisely where the late Nigel Tebbel bought his cigars. May I take one?"

Hargreave presented one of the cheap cigars to Holmes with a flourish. "Not an especially appealing variety, Holmes."

"But not ordinary, either," replied Holmes, sniffing the long tan cigar as if he were preparing to smoke it. "A touch of Cuban, mostly Virginian, decidedly domestic, about a penny a piece, I would presume. One other favour, Hargreave? Another look at that hotel key?"

"Of course," smiled Hargreave, handing it over. "Is it as

extraordinary as the cigar?"

"It has its interesting aspects, though I could tell you more if I had my magnifying glass with me, but it is in my rooms."

"Which are nearby," I suggested.

Holmes managed a small smile. "Two blocks walking," he remarked. "I could be there and back in a few minutes, including the time I would require to closely examine the key."

"I expect to be detained here for a time. I must have a chat with the witnesses, supervise the search of this area for a possible weapon," said Hargreave, eyeing the murder scene.

"You won't find it, of course," asserted Holmes.

"But we must have a look nonetheless," shrugged Hargreave. "Take the key, examine it."

"Excellent," replied Holmes. "And you, Teddy? Care to come along to my digs?"

"Well, yes, I would like that," I said emphatically.

Once inside his rooms, Holmes strode directly to a large corner work table that appeared to me to be burdened to the point of collapse with scientific paraphernalia – beakers, flasks, a microscope, piles of notebooks and an amazing array of bottles of various chemicals. From the midst of this clutter, he withdrew a large magnifying glass which he proceeded to use for a close look at the key he had carried snugly in his waistcoat pocket. Utterly ignored by the lean, intense young man bent over his table, I took the opportunity to have a look around his rooms.

That a man with such an orderly mind could permit his house to be so unkempt—a clutter of old newspapers, magazines, heaps of books – left me aghast, so much so that I, being a neat person, began tidying up, closing a book here and there, straightening piles of periodicals. Without looking away from his glass, Holmes announced brusquely, "Please touch nothing, Teddy!"

Startled, I drew back. "Sorry."

"Every item is where I want it to be. It may look a mess, but it has its own special order about it."

Chastened, I sank into the only chair not heaped with papers. "Can an ordinary key be that interesting?" I asked presently, peering across the clutter.

"It tells a story of its own. Come! See for yourself. You can readily tell that it is an old-style key, almost an antique. Dating from the ante-bellum period of your country's history, no doubt. The key is made of an alloy the chemistry of which has been refined by metal makers since this key was cast. The number has been gouged into it by the tip of a knife. A pocketknife, probably. The room to which it provides access has hardly been unoccupied for decades. Hundreds of uses have given the metal a very smooth patina. The lock which it opens has been quite defective for a long time. Any self-respecting burglar could get into that room in a trice. But you see all that, of course?"

"You amaze me, Holmes. How can you know so much from a key?"

"Ah, but I know far more than I've told you. Principally, I now know that we must look for a hotel very near the waterfront, a structure of no more than four floors, a bit dilapidated, probably a home for sailors or, perhaps, a lodging house for those unfortunate derelicts who have fallen on hard times through an addiction to drink or drugs. In short, Roosevelt, an establishment that is only a cut above what you New Yorkers quaintly call a flophouse."

"Astounding!"

"It's all here in the key," he smiled, dropping the object into my palm. "Notice the discoloration from corrosion that could come only from years of exposure to the damp air that one finds at the waterfront. Add to that my dating of the key as pre-Civil War, and you must deduce that the building that belongs to this key predates the taller ones that are becoming the fashion and the wave of the future for Manhattan, which is an island and which will, surely, have to build upward once it expands to occupy all available land for erecting structures."

"But how can you say that this hotel is a cut above being a flophouse?"

"Because," he smiled, reaching into his breast pocket and withdrawing Tebbel's cheap cigar, "it has the civilised amenity of a cigar stand on its premises."

"Obviously," I smiled.

"Obviously," nodded Holmes. "Now, back to the scene of the crime, eh?"

A wagon from Bellevue Hospital stood in the middle of the street as we approached the Tilden house once more. Hargreave, hatless against the drizzle, appeared to be in animated conversation with a young man holding an umbrella in one hand, which also held a pad upon which he was trying to write with a pencil held in his other hand. The two men paused in their discussion to observe the attendants in white coats placing the shrouded corpse of Nigel Tebbel into the wagon.

"I see that the press has finally put in an appearance," commented Holmes as we crossed the wet street toward Hargreave and the young man with pad and umbrella.

"That is all I have to tell you," Hargreave was saying firmly to the reporter.

"May I ask who these gentlemen are?" asked the reporter as Holmes and I approached.

"Theodore Roosevelt," said I, "and this is…"

"William Escott," said Holmes abruptly.

"Are you with the police?" asked the reporter.

"We are not," said Holmes.

"We had been at dinner with Hargreave when he was called here," I explained. I was cut off sharply by Holmes.

"I assure you we are of no interest to you whatever, young man," he announced, leading me by the arm away from the newspaperman.

"All other information will have to come from Mulberry Street," announced Hargreave, also turning away from the youth, who lingered for a few moments until he realised he would learn nothing more from us, even by eavesdropping.

"And what have you learned by your examination of the key, Mr Holmes?" whispered Hargreave.

"It has some interesting aspects," said Holmes, "but forgive me if I withhold a complete answer to your question until I have had more time to consider those aspects."

Hargreave smiled. "A dead end, eh?"

"In criminal investigations there is no such thing as a dead end," replied Holmes, "there are only indications that one's efforts ought to be directed another way. Will there be an autopsy in this case?"

"Yes."

"May I be privy to its findings?"

"I expect that we know all we need to know about how Mr Tebbel died."

"In all probability. Still, it would be instructive to know the pathologist's findings."

"I'll keep you informed," said Hargreave.

"And let me know when you have confirmation that the tin of powder is cocaine. Now, you have your duties to perform, so Roosevelt and I will bid you goodnight."

Holmes moved purposefully toward the nearby corner of Fourth Avenue and Twentieth Street and I hurried after him to the corner, which was familiar to me by virtue of the fact that my boyhood home was half a block distant. At the curb, Holmes turned to me with a look from his steel-grey eyes that I was beginning to recognise as his most compelling physical characteristic, far more riveting of one's attention than that hawk nose, the thin face, the prominent chin. "Are you a day person or a night person, Roosevelt?" he asked.

"I beg your pardon?"

"It is getting on to midnight. I wonder if you are eagerly anticipating the embrace of Morpheus, or are you a young man who doesn't mind an occasional late night?"

"I sleep as little as possible, it being my belief that there is too much to accomplish in life to waste time in slumber."

"Bravo. I thought as much. You will accompany me, then?"

"Where?"

"In search of all there is to know about the late Nigel Tebbel. I assure you, before dawn breaks over this restless city, you and I will know Tebbel's home, his haunts, the kind of man he was, the company he kept. Knowing all of this, we will soon know who killed Nigel Tebbel and why."

"Where do we begin?"

"With our hack that is so rapidly approaching and telling the driver to take us to 53 Warren Street."

"Tell me, Holmes," I said as we settled in the hack and moved smartly downtown through the damp and nearly deserted streets, "how can you be so certain that the powder in that tin was cocaine?"

"I am quite familiar with the drug, Roosevelt."

"Is there anything you have not studied?"

"Very little, thank you."

"And what are we to find at Warren Street. The number you gave to the hackie was 53, I believe?"

"Precisely."

"The hotel to which that key belonged?"

Holmes looked at me sidewise with a smile. "You give me too much credit. The location of Tebbel's hotel remains a mystery. What we will find at 53 Warren Street is St Vincent's Home for Newsboys, a remarkable institution established and run by one of the most fascinating men of the cloth it has ever been my pleasure to meet – Father John Christopher Drumgoole."

Six

F ather Drumgoole," explained Holmes, "came to New York as an immigrant from Ireland. Like the thousands who, even today, are pouring through America's open and welcoming door, Drumgoole was a penniless young fellow for whom his native land had lost all promise. Much of his life in New York he spent as a janitor in the many Roman Catholic churches of this city. In his adult years, he decided he had a calling to the priesthood and, after diligently applying himself at seminary, he earned his cassock. He took a particular interest in the plight of the homeless and hungry boys who were trying to keep themselves alive by selling penny newspapers. That is a hard life, Roosevelt! The lads must buy the newspapers themselves and hawk them as best they can, praying to get rid of every one, because what they buy they keep. You cannot walk the streets of this city without finding these newsboys sleeping in doorways or spending their pennies in the saloons that cater to them."

"Saloons for children?" I cried. "What kind of persons would sell alcoholic beverages to children?"

"Greedy persons with no scruples whatsoever," replied Holmes.

"Something should be done about it!"

"Something will be done when political men have the courage required to do the job."

"Father Drumgoole, then, took pity on these lads?" I asked.

"By establishing the St Vincent's Home to which we are going."

"Yet I fail to see the purpose of our visit," I confessed.

"I am going to enlist the aid of a few of the lads who have been helpful to me in the past on small problems that have engaged my spare time since I came to New York. One of the youngsters, who is the natural leader of my small army of irregulars in the war against crime, was especially useful in the Vanderbilt problem a few months ago. The lad is named James Wakefield. A bright fellow for whom there could be a career with the police force if he would apply himself. I have been encouraging him along those lines."

"You are an amazing man, Holmes – recruiting newsboys in the fight against crime!"

"And what better assistants could there be? They are more familiar with the streets, saloons, and alleys of New York than any roundsman of Hargreave's constabulary. These lads have the distinct advantage of being easily overlooked. They are so miserable, so far down on the rungs of the ladder of our civilisation that they are never noticed. It is as if they did not exist. As a result, things are done and said with them as witnesses that would never happen, never be said, were adults within seeing or hearing distance."

Presently, we arrived at Father Drumgoole's enterprise and, inside, found ourselves surrounded by a throng of the lads who noisily and warmly greeted Holmes for the friend he seemed to be. In a moment, the extraordinary Father Drumgoole was at our sides, his ruddy Irish face aglow with pleasure, a heavy chain with a crucifix about his neck, his cassock rakishly open at the collar. "Holmes, what a surprise to see you so soon," he exclaimed, offering a big, calloused hand to his visitor.

"May I introduce Mr Theodore Roosevelt?" said Holmes, directing the priest's attention to me.

"The Roosevelt family have been generous in their support of my work," said the priest, "though I have not had the pleasure of meeting this member of the family."

"We are a large clan," I said, taking the priest's strong hand in mine. "I have plenty of uncles, aunts, and cousins."

"Is Wakefield on the premises?" asked Holmes.

"He'll be here in a moment," said Father Drumgoole, leading us away from the milling throng of admiring boys to the study of the Home. Presently, we were joined by the lad Wakefield – a youth of, I surmised, fifteen years, who greeted Holmes with an admiring and bright smile beneath mischievous blue eyes. His blond hair curled over the collar of his blue jacket, which appeared about one size too small for him.

"You've grown a full inch since last we met," said Holmes, clapping the boy on his broad shoulders. "Say hello to my friend Roosevelt."

"Pleased to meetcha," said the youth with a courtly bow of the head.

"Roosevelt and I are on an interesting problem," said Holmes, taking the youth by the arm and directing him to one of the chairs in the cosy book-lined study while Father Drumgoole stood aside, listening. "We must determine the haunts of a certain Nigel Tebbel, whom I take to be a cocaine user."

"There's enough of them around," remarked the lad with a decisive nod of his head.

"It is vital that I know when this Tebbel fellow was last seen in his usual haunts and where I might locate persons who know him."

"You want me and the lads to find this Tebbel for you?" asked young Wakefield.

"Tebbel is dead," stated Holmes.

"Somebody done him in?" asked the boy.

"A short time ago in Gramercy Park," nodded Holmes.

"My word," muttered Father Drumgoole. "May the Lord have mercy on his soul. I will include his name in the Mass tomorrow."

"I suspect Tebbel will need all the prayers he can get," commented Holmes.

"A cocaine user, you say," said Wakefield.

"He had a quantity of it in a small tin," I ventured.

"The fellow must have money to have his own supply of cocaine with him," said the lad.

"Why do you say that?" I asked.

"Most cocaine takers do it in opium dens," he replied with assurance. I must have exhibited on my face the surprise I felt at the lad's intimate knowledge of so sordid a business because the youth grinned. "Mr Roosevelt doesn't know much about these things, eh, Mr Holmes?" he commented.

"As a matter of fact, Tebbel had a large sum of money on him when he was murdered," Holmes said. "Yet he hardly seemed a rich man."

"Struck it rich lately?" asked Wakefield.

"Apparently," replied Holmes.

"Rich enough to get himself a supply of cocaine. Must be some job he did for that kind of money," Wakefield observed.

"Good for you, lad!" said Holmes, clapping his hands with delight. "You see the point exactly! Tebbel was obviously hired to do something, paid a large amount of money for it, then either failed to do it…"

"Or fouled it up doing it," added Wakefield.

"Collecting a bullet in the back as his reward and punishment," Holmes stated coldly.

"My word!" gasped Father Drumgoole, dropping into his spacious chair behind his cluttered desk.

"If this Tebbel was a cocaine user there are a dozen places where he would have gone before he struck it rich enough to get his own supply," Wakefield explained thoughtfully.

"I believe he would have frequented a den close to the waterfront," said Holmes. With a sidewise glance at me he added, "The key, Roosevelt. You see?"

"The corroded condition of it," I nodded.

"The waterfront," mused Wakefield, his boyish brow creased with the pondering of this information. "That narrows it down to three or four places. Shall we get to work on this right now, Mr Holmes?"

Holmes turned to Father Drumgoole. The priest frowned, chewed his lip, drummed his fingertips upon his desktop, and noted, "I require the boys to observe a strict curfew, Mr Holmes."

"I understand," said Holmes, clearly disappointed at this decision by the priest.

"Surely this job can wait until tomorrow," said the priest.

"Father," said Wakefield, "I don't believe Mr Holmes would have come here at this hour if this wasn't something darned important."

"Is that right, Mr Holmes?" asked the priest.

"I would not be overstating the urgency, Father Drumgoole, if I were to tell you that this is a case with sinister and far-reaching implications."

"That important, eh?"

"It is of the most serious nature, Father Drumgoole. Lives are at stake, one of them the life of a man of critical importance."

"Well, with lives at stake," muttered the priest.

Urgently, Holmes rose from his chair and leaned across the priest's desk. "John, I have never come to you and your boys for assistance in anything that was not of the greatest moment, but I assure you that the importance of all those other cases dwindles to nothingness in the face of this current problem."

Against this astounding statement from Sherlock Holmes, Father Drumgoole stood little chance of prevailing. Indeed, who would not have acceded to Holmes in view of what he had so urgently stated – to my amazement, because I had no clue as to what had led Holmes to make these startling utterances. "Very well," said the priest, throwing up his hands in surrender.

"Hooray!" cried Wakefield.

"On your way," said Holmes. "I want you to deliver a message which I am going to write if Father Drumgoole will lend me his pen? The address is 24 State Street."

"Not far from here," nodded Wakefield, taking the note and slipping it into his pocket.

"I will be at my lodgings on Twenty-second Street," said Holmes. "You know what it is I need to know, Wakefield?"

"Indeed I do," said the lad enthusiastically.

"Off, then," said Holmes.

At which, Wakefield darted from the room the way an ordinary boy would have if he had been told there were cookies and cider in the kitchen. A group of his young companions joined him enthusiastically – and noisily – but in a moment's time, the pack of irregulars was gone, disappeared into a nighttime city which they obviously knew exceedingly well.

After a farewell to Father Drumgoole at the door, Holmes and I climbed into our cab. "I had no idea that this case was as important as you have made it seem," I remarked as we turned north onto Broadway.

"It is the most serious case I have yet encountered, Roosevelt, either in England or here in America."

Protestations that he could not leave me without an explanation of this sensational remark failed to elicit further words from him except for him to assure me that he was in dead earnest, adding, "From this point, I believe it would be best if you leave this problem to me."

"Really, Mr Sherlock Holmes," I protested, "if you think you can bring me along this far and dump me at my doorstep, you are mistaken. I'm in this to the finish."

Holmes laughed. "Good show, Teddy! I was hoping you would say that! Very well. Be prepared for an early rising, for I believe I shall have news from Wakefield soon. Then you and I will see where the discoveries lead us."

"But you must get your rest," I suggested.

"I will not rest until this case is resolved," he stated. "I have this night and all day tomorrow to resolve it, and, if all goes as I expect, I shall have put this case behind us in time for tomorrow evening's performance of *Twelfth Night*. You seem surprised."

"Who would not be at hearing such a confident boast?"

"It is not a boast, Roosevelt, but a promise, for this is a matter in which time is of the essence. Now, goodnight."

Seven

To my astonishment, Holmes was back at my door in less than two hours' time. "The game's afoot! Wakefield, that remarkable boy, has located a man we must see immediately. If you wish to accompany me, dress accordingly. We are going to The Five Points section of this city, as dismal a cesspool of humanity as one may find anywhere, including my London. It is infested with thieves, murderers, rowdies of every stripe, prostitutes, drunkards, and cutthroats. It has and deserves a reputation as the most evil section of New York. Hargreave remarked that you are handy with firearms. I suggest you bring along a pistol."

"Really, Holmes, I don't think even The Five Points neighbourhood is so dangerous that a pair of strong and courageous men such as we need arms. I have always believed that even if you put the best weapon that can be invented in the hands of a coward, as these persons of The Five Points surely are, he will be beaten by a brave man unarmed."

"Well said, Teddy, but bring along your revolver anyway."

In our carriage, Holmes was once more withdrawn and contemplative, the same Holmes who had sat at my side during the drive from the Hoffman House to Gramercy Park. The aquiline face was flushed with excitement, the brows drawn together into a dark line above hard eyes that glinted like cold steel. He was as taut and ready as a hound on the scent, which, I realised, was precisely the case. Presently, we turned into the dark streets of the sinister neighbourhood called The Five Points. Unlike other neighborhoods through which we had passed on our way – quiet and peaceful as the residents slumbered safely in their beds – this region was crawling with shadowy figures scurrying here and there, nighttime creatures who were alert and alive only in the dark. "What a miserable pack they are," I muttered, nodding toward a knot of ruffians in hushed conspiracy beneath a lamp.

Holmes stirred to glance at the men in the dim light. "Yes," he sighed, turning away again, "they are dirty-looking rascals, but as low and loathsome as they are, each has a spark of immortality about him. You would not think it to look at them, of course, but they are men with souls. Ah, man! What an enigma he is!"

"Thieves, one and all," I responded sourly. "Pathetic!"

"Isn't all of life exactly that? Futile? Pathetic? We reach and what have we in our grasp at the end of life? A shadow."

"A miserable neighbourhood, this," I stated with disgust, but that disgust quickly gave way to pity. "I am a religious man, Holmes, but at times I must ask myself what purpose such misery can serve."

"That is the one problem which human reason has never answered," replied Holmes. "I doubt it ever will. That is a question of religion. Oh, yes, I am a religious man, as well.

I reject the proposition that our universe is ruled by chance. I see by your expression that I surprise you, yet there is nothing in which deduction is so necessary as religion. I long ago deduced the existence of Providence from a rose. Yes, a rose. A splendid bloom it was and, as I studied it, I saw immediately that the highest assurance of the goodness of Providence was found in the very existence of that flower. All other things are really necessary for our existence. But the rose is extra, an embellishment to life, not a condition of life. It could only be goodness which gives such extras, the goodness of Providence. Ah, here we are! Driver. Pull up here!"

I peered through the pitch-black night at the grimy facade of a saloon with the improbable name The Peaceful Glade. The wooden sign bearing the name of the establishment was badly weathered, the paint chipped and faded and nearly illegible in the flicker of the lamp above it. The building itself was a two-storey affair of brick whose red colour was encrusted with an accumulation of black soot and green slime – deposits from the effluence of hundreds of chimneys and the mists from the nearby East River through the decades. As Holmes and I stood before this revolting place, I slipped my hand into my pocket to find the reassuring cold steel of my revolver. "A nurturing place for how many crimes?" I muttered as we crossed the wet sidewalk.

Holmes, peering amusedly at me from beneath the brim of his cap, replied, "The vilest alleys of a city do not present a more dreadful record of sin than does the smiling countryside, Roosevelt!"

As he pushed open the door of The Peaceful Glade with a remarkable sense of belonging, I followed close behind, trying to emulate his confidence, but bolstered by the gun beneath my pocketed hand. "What a smell," I whispered as we stepped into the stench of years of whiskey and tobacco smoke. The large room which we entered by way of a small descending staircase was only barely brighter than the night outside. In the glow of kerosene lamps and candles upon tables that crowded the room I felt that every eye in the establishment was fixed upon Holmes and me. Although I had put on my most casual sporting clothes in keeping with the informal attire which Holmes was wearing, I felt decidedly overdressed. I might as well have worn evening clothes, for my clothing stood out like a sore thumb among the shabby adornment of the denizens of that place.

As Holmes stepped up to the bar, two surly, sinister-looking men made room for him grudgingly. "A man named Griggs?" asked Holmes of the barman.

"Who're you and whatcha want with Griggs?" demanded the burly fellow.

"Who I am and my business with Griggs are none of your affair," replied Holmes sharply.

"A copper, eh?"

"If I am and you aren't more cooperative you will find the shutters closed upon this establishment quicker than boiled asparagus!"

"Griggs, you say?"

"Griggs!"

"In the back," nodded the barman with decidedly more respect.

"You certainly intimidated that fellow by making him believe you were with the police," I whispered, chuckling with admiration.

"It has long been a maxim of mine, Teddy, that nothing is more important than making people believe what you wish them to believe."

"Who is this fellow Griggs?"

"None other than the half brother of the late Nigel Tebbel," he stated, threading through the clutter of tables, chairs, and customers to a small table in a dark corner where sat a man whose suspicious eyes had followed our progress step by step. "Griggs, I have bad news for you," stated Holmes without preliminaries as he stepped up to the bottle-strewn table. Griggs stared at the tall intruder for a moment, then lowered his gaze to his folded hands – rough, calloused, and scarred, the hands of a man who had probably worked years as a stevedore on nearby wharves.

"Your half brother is dead," Holmes said quietly.

Griggs nodded slowly and brushed a finger beneath his florid nose. "I warned him," he muttered, his voice choking back an unexpected emotion.

Holmes drew up chairs for himself and for me. As we sat, he asked, "You warned him that he might be killed?"

Griggs shook his head slowly, evidently trying to hold back tears that would have seemed singularly out of place in that dismal establishment of rowdy laughter and noisy song. "I warned Nige that he ought not have anything to do with uptown swells. They could only spell trouble, I told him."

"Who were these uptown swells?" asked Holmes.

"Dunno," grunted Griggs, adding gruffly, "and who the hell are you to be comin' in here and askin about Nige? A copper?"

"I am not with the police," Holmes quietly assured him.

"Then git the hell outta here."

"Have you no interest in apprehending the murderers of your half brother?" I demanded.

Griggs turned hard and angry blue eyes toward me. "He's dead and that's all there is to that."

"But, surely, man…"

Holmes cut me off with a glance. Turning back to Griggs, he asked, "In what regiment did you serve in the Civil War?"

"The Seventh New York," Griggs replied, his face amazed. "How'd you know about me bein' in the war?"

"A small tattoo, the edge of which I can see plainly beneath the edge of your sleeve cuff. It is, if I am not in error, a rendering of a victorious Columbia. The tattoo was quite popular among merchant seamen who were veterans of the war. I take it that after the conflict you went to sea?"

"You have a sharp eye and a shrewd brain, sir," muttered Griggs.

"You must have been quite young at the time of the war," I suggested.

"I was a drummer boy," said Griggs, lifting his shoulders proudly. "Twelve years old, I was. My Pa was in the same regiment. He got killed at Chancellorsville. After the war, my Ma married again, but her second husband was a rounder and a rascal and absconded, leaving Ma with the little boy Nigel and no man to care for them."

"So you gave up the sea and began working as a stevedore," stated Holmes.

"Yes. Thanks be to God Ma is gone and won't have to suffer knowing Nigel 'as been murdered."

"In memory of her you should cooperate with us," I said sympathetically.

"And wind up dead myself? No thank you."

"In that case I must appeal to your obvious patriotism, Griggs—that same patriotism that stirred you to come to the aid of your country in the Civil War and to have that tattoo in memory of victory. I appeal to the sense of duty which you exhibited in giving up your career as a seaman to aid your widowed mother. I must tell you, Griggs, that your brother was the victim of a group of ruthless individuals who mean harm to your country."

Griggs lifted his reddening eyes to Holmes. "What do you mean, sir?"

"I mean that your brother was killed by men who will stop at nothing to achieve their ends. Your brother appears to have crossed them. So, they murdered him. If you have any feeling for him, for your martyred father, for your mother, for your country, then you must help me if I am to prevent further disasters."

"What could I possibly say to help you?"

"I need to know your brother's whereabouts yesterday and earlier this evening."

Griggs shrugged. "I can't help you. I ain't seen him in two, three days."

"Where did he live?"

"A hotel on the west side of the city."

"Near the waterfront?" asked Holmes.

"Yeah. A place on West Street."

"The address?"

"Dunno."

"Your brother was a cocaine user! Did he frequent any special dens on the west side?"

Overwhelmed by the realisation that Holmes knew a great deal about his brother, Griggs slumped in his chair and toyed with his whiskey glass, his head down to his chest, his voice barely audible above the din of that awful place. "You even know about Nigel's addiction to that hellish powder? I tried many times to show 'im the error of his ways, and while Ma was alive there was some hope for 'im. But when she died of the consumption disease there was nothing I could do to keep Nige from gettin' into the worst possible kinds of trouble."

"What sort of trouble?" I asked.

"Rowdyin', mostly. He was a strong lad all his life. Got that from his Pa, I suppose. Nigel was always in scrapes of one kind or another and before long he was hirin' himself out to whoever needed a man who could use his fists or a club or a knife, if it came to that. You would be surprised, gentlemen, at the number of persons of your class who come down to these miserable streets lookin' for someone like my brother to do their dirty work for 'em. Especially when there's an election comin' up."

"This was the kind of work your brother did, then," said Holmes. "Hiring out as a tough and a strong-arm man, but with special interest in brutalising and intimidating voters going to the polls?"

Griggs nodded sadly. "It is not a pretty story, I know, but Nigel needed a great deal of money to feed his addiction, you see."

"Yes, I see," said Holmes, "and I regret that your brother came to such a bad end, but if it can be of any comfort at a time like this, I must express my belief that your brother's ill fate should not rest upon your conscience. From what you have said I am convinced you did all you could to rescue your brother's life."

"That's very kind of you, sir," muttered Griggs, choking back his tears.

"I have one more question, Griggs. Then my associate and I will leave you to find the peace you deserve. Had your brother been active as a strong-arm man in the most recent Presidential election?"

Griggs nodded slowly.

"On whose behalf?" asked Holmes.

"A fellow I knew only as Charles hired Nige to beat up people who were going to the voting places to cast their ballots for Tilden."

"What a dastardly thing!" I exclaimed.

"Charles, you say?" asked Holmes, glancing at me with the light of discovery in his grey eyes. "The initials on the scrap of paper, Roosevelt. C. G."

"You know this Charles?" asked Griggs.

"No, but I hope to meet him soon," said Holmes.

"Well, he's a bad one, and you would be wise if you took precautions. Yet bad as Charles is, he pals around with another bully who's worse. Don't know his name, but you would not fail to see him in a crowd. A giant man with flaming red hair and beard and the look of a madman in his eyes."

"What a remarkable fellow you are, Griggs," cried Holmes. "Can you describe the man called Charles?"

"A mousy young fellow. Brown hair, wispy whiskers, a face that's kind of thin, like he ain't had a good meal in a long time. A sullen son of a—"

"Yes," nodded Holmes. "A small man?"

"I would guess about five-five. Skinny, too. Gave me the creeps, he did, him in his black suit and one of those slouched hats that people who want to hide their faces wear."

"Thank you, Griggs," announced Holmes. "You have been most helpful."

Once again in the fresher air in front of The Peaceful Glade, I surveyed the street for a cab to take us out of that dreadful neighbourhood. "It is a curious coincidence," I remarked, "that Tebbel died in front of the residence of the man whom he worked against in the election of '76 to the point of brutalising Tilden voters."

"Coincidence, Roosevelt? Hardly! When a man who was hired to terrorise Tilden voters is shot to death on Tilden's doorstep the bounds of coincidence are stretched too far! You will recall that I pointed out at the scene of the crime that it appeared obvious that Tebbel was trying to reach Tilden's house at the very moment of his death."

"But why? We have just heard that Tebbel worked against Tilden."

"Yes."

"It makes no sense."

"Yet I assure you, Roosevelt, there is a sense to it, and you and I will discern it. I promise you that! Now, if we may hail this hack, while I accompany you to your home, you may be of great assistance to me by discoursing on the details of the election of 1876, which seems to be playing an increasingly important part in our fancy little problem."

Eight

As I have told you, my brother Mycroft is the Holmes who has the interest in and the understanding of political matters," continued Holmes as we settled into our cab, "but I am fortunate in this affair to have you to fill the shoes of Mycroft, given your own interest in and knowledge of politics. Pray, educate me!"

Sherlock Holmes proved an excellent student, listening to me intently and making few interruptions for questions as our hack plodded uptown toward my residence. "As you may or may not know, Holmes, the American political system has evolved into a two-party system. There are what we call splinter parties, of course, but they attract little support at the polls. The major parties, the Democrats and the Republicans, encompass the vast majority of the American electorate. Yet within the two parties there are factions which often feud with each other, coming together only after the moment when a slate of candidates has been chosen. This intra-party factionalism can be very bitter. We have witnessed a recent example of it within the Republican party, even though the Republicans have their man in the Executive Mansion in the form of Rutherford B. Hayes. I will say more about the Republicans in a moment.

"First, let me tell you about that remarkable gentleman, Governor Samuel Jones Tilden, and the events which led to him being selected as the Democratic candidate for President of the United States in 1876, just four years ago. Governor Tilden is a man of unquestioned integrity and moral uprightness who came to national prominence as a reformer who overthrew the notorious Tweed Ring."

A sidewise glance at Holmes indicated to me that he had no knowledge of the infamous Tweed Ring, and I found it prudent to digress from my comments upon Tilden to explain the basic function of political machines in America's large cities. "Tweed, that is William Tweed," I explained, "is the boss of the faction of the Democratic party known as Tammany Hall. In New York City, as in other great cities, political affairs occasionally fall under the direction of a class of men who make politics their regular business and means of livelihood. These men do this successfully because they are able to organise their respective parties or factions. These organisations have come to be called machines, and they serve some very important roles in our country – helping those who need help, providing social services to the poor, and stimulating interest in elections. Machines are not entirely anathema, you see. Well, the career of 'Boss' Tweed is a singular example of how these salutary characteristics of machines combined with the vilest type of bossism that results in the hiring of men like Tebbel as thugs to intimidate and terrorise the political opposition both in the other party and within the machine's party. Tilden was instrumental in opposing the Tweed Ring, as I have said.

"Because of his success, four years ago Tilden was chosen as the Democratic choice for President. Tilden was, at the time, governor of New York. The campaign was to be a bitter one and the chief issue in the debate was corruption. Both parties accused each other of it.

"Until the Republicans met in convention, it was expected that they would nominate as their standard-bearer James G. Blaine of Maine. The Republicans would have much preferred, I believe, to nominate President Grant once more, but there is an unwritten rule in American politics that no President may run for a third term. This is based on the refusal of Washington to do so, and every President since has followed Washington's example. I do not believe the American people will ever permit a President to hold office for more than eight years.

"Unable to name Grant, the Republicans found themselves in heated debate over choosing a successor. Ohio delegates quite understandably went to the convention in support of their favourite son, Mr Hayes, although the national party leadership looked with favour on Blaine. Well, American politics is rarely predictable, and after six ballots, the Republicans still had no candidate. On the seventh, Hayes emerged from obscurity and he was nominated.

"Then came the campaign, and it was unmatched in its ugliness. It was expected that Tilden would win. Indeed, the headlines on the morning after the election announced Tilden *was* the winner. Popular votes clearly gave it to Tilden as did electoral votes. Do you know about our Electoral College?"

"It is familiar to me," nodded Holmes. "I recall remarking to Mycroft that it seems odd to me that this system of assigning electoral votes to states on the basis of their Congressional representation might deny the majority of voters their choice."

"It was through this very electoral system that the Republicans were able to challenge the outcome of the election, claiming that in certain Southern states Negroes were denied their vote. The outcome of the balloting was upset and the election was thrown to Hayes. Yet despite this, the certification of the voting was still in doubt because the Congress consisted of a Democratic House and a Republican Senate. Our democracy was at an impasse. Three months of extreme unrest followed amid virulent accusations of election fraud. Mr. Charles Dana of the *Sun* even to this day refers to President Hayes as 'His Fraudulency!'"

"I've been amazed at the libellous things Mr Dana says in his newspaper."

"The *Sun* has contributed greatly to the poisoning of the political process."

"And how was the contested election of 1876 resolved?"

"By a compromise. A special commission was set up consisting of five members from the House, five from the Senate, and five from the Supreme Court. However, this seemingly impartial panel was in fact weighted to the Republicans because three of the five Justices were Republicans. The commission, therefore, decided for the Republicans. To get this result approved by the House, Mr Hayes promised Democrats that he would, once in office, remove federal troops from Southern states, assuring Democrats of future electoral victories in that region. Tilden acquiesced in a gentlemanly way and this seemed to still the political tempests, but now another Presidential election is upon us and the Republicans are again engaged in bitter controversies. One faction wanted to nominate Grant again, believing that the intervening four years since the end of his second term eliminated the 'third term' problem. Here in New York, the Grant faction calls itself the Stalwarts. These men are angry with Hayes for his civil service reforms, in which he went so far as to remove Chester Arthur as Collector of the Port of New York, a rich political patronage position. Supporters of Blaine are called Half-Breeds, and they proved to be decisive in the recent Republican convention. The Half-Breeds switched from Blaine to James A. Garfield, who was nominated as the Republican candidate at the convention in Chicago a fortnight ago. To assuage the Stalwarts, the convention chose Arthur as the Vice-Presidential candidate."

"Whom have the Democrats chosen?" asked Holmes.

"A war hero, Major General Winfield Scott Hancock, a fellow with no real political experience but, as I stated, a hero by virtue of his soldiering at Gettysburg."

"Your political parties have a penchant for assuming that heroic generals are suited to be political leaders," Holmes remarked, sourly.

"Not without some justification," I replied to this criticism. "I give you Washington and Jackson!"

"Are you able to predict for me the outcome of the present contest?" Holmes asked with a slight smile.

"My prediction would be tainted by my own political bias. I am a Republican."

"So you will vote for Garfield?"

"It is the glory of the American political system that how a man votes is a secret," I chuckled.

"A splendid arrangement," nodded Holmes. "Borrowed from the English!"

"Our hack has arrived at my doorstep," I pointed out, "and I have completed my thumbnail sketch of recent American political events. I trust it was useful to you."

"Indeed," said Holmes, opening the door to the hack for me to step down. "It has been most instructive."

"And what is the next step in our current problem?" I asked.

"To bed," he said with a very surprising wink. "But I shall be up early and if you'd like, I'll send for you when I make my next move."

"I would never forgive you if you did not," I replied.

"Good night, then," he waved. As his hack sprang away into the night, the sky was already showing tinges of approaching dawn.

The rain was over, I noted as I ascended the steps to my door in anticipation of, at least, a few hours' rest.

Nine

It proved a folly on my part to believe that I could sleep in the excited state of my mind following the extraordinary events of the night. Rather, I retired to my library where, beneath the glow of my desk lamp and in the brightening light of dawn through the windows, I jotted notes on all that had transpired with, I confess, the hope that I might find in the collection of data the sort of information which Mr Sherlock Holmes might use to deduce the answer to the confounded riddle of Nigel Tebbel and the events of his death in such a singular and tragic manner.

My manner of detective work resembled that of a book-keeper as I divided a sheet of paper into two columns, one to list the facts as we knew them, one to list the questions which remained unanswered:

The Facts as Known in the Murder of Tebbel

1. Shot to death at #15 Gramercy Park South, the home of Tilden.

2. Robbery not motive – no money taken.

3. Clues: cigars, tin of cocaine, paper with letters *C* and *G* upon it, hotel room key.

4. Tebbel was political bully and ruffian.

5. Had been hired to do some dirty work — this is an assumption rather than arrived at by evidence.

6. Not seen for few days by his half brother.

7. The brother referred to a mysterious man named Charles as being connected with Tebbel.

Unanswered Questions in Death of Tebbel

1. Why was he killed?

2. Who killed him?

3. What mission was he engaged upon?

4. Location of hotel to which key belongs.

5. What was Tebbel doing in Gram. Pk.?

6. Meaning of letters C and G.

7. Does the C represent the mysterious Charles?

With a chuckle I noted that my columns were equal — a tidy balance, as if I had, indeed, been playing accountant rather than detective.

I was mulling over my lists and having a light breakfast when Hargreave appeared at the door, to be shown into the dining room by the butler. "You are up bright and early," said Will with a cheery nod.

"I have not been to bed! Holmes and I spent the night visiting some of the most remarkable places you could imagine!"

"I gathered that from this message which I received at 300 Mulberry Street this morning," said Will, passing me a note in Holmes' hand: "Please come to my rooms at No. 39 East 22d St. I have information of the most vital nature. Bring R. along when you come. I will be waiting for you precisely at ten. S. H."

"What do you make of it?" I asked, returning the note.

"I have not the vaguest notion, but it is a quarter to ten," replied Hargreave, fishing out his pocketwatch.

We were at Holmes' doorstep exactly at ten and were admitted immediately, although both Hargreave and I were taken aback by Holmes' appearance, which was that of a merchant seaman – blue cap, striped shirt, workaday trousers, boots. Yet this clothing was not half as startling as his face, which sported what seemed to be a beard of a few weeks' growth while below his right eye a livid scar crossed the cheek from nose to ear. "You are certainly prompt," he remarked, "for I have just this instant returned."

"What an extraordinary sight you are!" I gasped.

"Yes. I am a passable seaman, eh?"

Hargreave was amused. "And may I ask the purpose of this get-up?"

Holmes closed the door and made room for us amid the clutter, tossing piles of materials to the floor to uncover chairs. "I have occasionally found the use of disguises helpful," he explained, removing the costume and makeup as deftly as he had shed the character of Malvolio. "In this, my work on the stage has been of vital importance. I confess my seaman's disguise is one of my favorites, although I have a little old flower lady who would win your hearts. I have located the hotel to which Tebbel's key belongs – a very disreputable establishment on West Street *directly opposite the ferry slip used by the North German Lloyds Steamship Company!*"

This news brought Hargreave and me from our chairs.

"I hasten to assure you that the President is quite safe! He is at the home of the United States Attorney, Mr Woodford, in Manhattan Beach. I had no time to inform you, Hargreave. The President changed his plans last night and remained aboard the ship until he could be taken by boat to Manhattan Beach. That was in accord with my suggestion."

"*Your* suggestion?"

"The President was in the gravest danger, I assure you, and there was no time for me to do anything but what I did. I confess that I broke one of my cardinal rules in this matter and took action on a conclusion to which I jumped without all the requisite supporting data. It was obvious to me from the beginning of this problem that a sinister political motive was at the root of Tebbel's murder. Having ruled out robbery as a motive I had to confront the evidence at hand, namely that Tebbel was killed to keep him from reaching the Tilden house. The presence of so much money on Tebbel's body indicated that he had been hired for some purpose. I assumed it was to commit some political act about which Tebbel got cold feet. Knowing Tilden's moral up-rightness, it was impossible for Tebbel to have been working for him, so it followed that he was working for someone else and that, changing his mind about his role in the affair, he turned to the only person he knew might be able to safely help him. Forgive me, Hargreave, but the New York police are not known for trustworthiness at this time."

"But how did you suspect a plot against Hayes?" I asked.

"That is where I had to jump to my conclusion even without all the facts," said Holmes with a puff on his calabash.

"I can see why you would make that assumption," said Hargreave. "If Tilden was not Tebbel's target, who was? Who is there in this city who might be the object of a plot?"

"The mayor," I stated emphatically.

"The mayor is, I believe, out of town," said Holmes.

"He is," said Hargreave.

"But the news of the President visiting the city had not been widely circulated," I pointed out.

"Yet it is safe to expect that conspirators would know," said Holmes.

"Who are these cowardly conspirators?" I demanded.

Holmes shrugged. "I cannot answer that part of the riddle, I'm afraid."

"How can we be sure the President is safe?" I asked.

"We can be sure he is safe at the moment, but we must now locate this conspiracy and root it out to ensure his future safety," Holmes nodded. "That is why I took the extraordinary step of advising those with the President to take the President elsewhere rather than return to Manhattan. Arrangements are being made for Mr Hayes to return to Washington this afternoon."

"How did you accomplish this, Holmes?" I asked, amazed at his audacity.

"You recall the message I gave to Wakefield to deliver?"

"I remember."

"It was to the British Consul General, an old friend of mine from my school days. He and I shared a dislike for a certain mathematics professor, one James Moriarty. The Consul General acted upon my advice by endorsing my note and arranging for it to be delivered to the President even as Mr Hayes was preparing to debark from the S.S. *Mosel*. The President, thereupon, waited until arrangements could be made to transfer him directly to Woodford's home by boat. Had he followed the original plan, he would have returned to Manhattan and come within the gunsight that was waiting for him in room 405 of that certain hotel on West Street. Rest easy, Hargreave. The conspirators have abandoned the room. I have already examined it."

"You found nothing?" Hargreave sighed.

"I didn't say that. I found a great deal, and if you will accompany me to the room, I will show you all that we have to go on."

"But any evidence may have been removed by now," said Hargreave excitedly.

"I took the precaution of having the roundsman in that neighbourhood stand guard at the door," Holmes replied, laying aside his pipe. "It was a singular thing for me to do, I confess – ordering about one of your constabulary, but when I explained that I was acting in your name and that you would be there presently, he undertook the duty willingly."

"By God, Holmes, you are an incredible fellow!" gasped Hargreave.

"But now we must see to it that these scurrilous conspirators are caught!" exclaimed Holmes, dashing for the door and the stairs.

Ten

Y ou observe the cigar stand in the lobby," said Holmes as he strode
through the door of the rundown hotel overlooking the Hudson
River waterfront. "It was Tebbel's cigar that led me here, as I knew it
would," he went on, leading Hargreave and me at a brisk pace up the
dim and dirty stairway to the fourth – the top – floor of the building.
"At the crack of dawn I paid a visit to a tobacco wholesale house on
Fulton Street to make enquiries as to where Tebbel's brand of cheap
cigars would be found at retail. I feared it would be a futile effort, given
the ordinariness of the product, but no! An astoundingly knowledgeable
fellow named Azerier, a superb tobacconist, said that while the brand
was common he knew of only a dozen or so retailers who handled the
product. From his list, I was able to narrow down my search by the
simple expedient of looking for addresses that were either hotels or near
to hotels and close to either of the city's rivers. I next consulted at the
Customs House as to what ships of the North German Lloyds line were
in port and where they might be berthed and discovered that this hotel
overlooks the ferry slip which must be used to get to the Hoboken dock

of the German company. It was Hargreave's mention of the President dining aboard a German steamer that gave me that tidbit of information. Having determined that Tebbel had to have visited this hotel, I came directly here, made my way unseen to the fourth floor, jemmied the lock to number 405, and went in. As I foretold, Roosevelt, it was an easy lock for a burglar to open! But we have no need to jemmy it because the door is unlocked, left that way by me under the watchful eyes of your roundsman, Hargreave."

The policeman saluted smartly upon recognising Hargreave as we came down the narrow corridor to 405, a small, square, sparely furnished room with a bed and a chest of drawers. Indeed, the only thing of immediate interest about it was its window, which was open. From it one was afforded an unobstructed view of the ferry slip used by the very steamship company which had been honoured the previous evening by a visit aboard one of its vessels by the President of the United States. The great German liner S.S. *Mosel* was clearly visible at its berth on the distant New Jersey shore. "My God," gasped Hargreave as he peered through the window, "the President would have been as easy to pick off as a sitting duck."

"Yes," nodded Holmes, "but the conspiracy has been thwarted, yet only for this day! We must now follow the clues that the room provides us in order to arrest this group of ruthless men before they have a chance to regroup and arrange a new plan."

"Clues?" I asked, my tone a mixture of anger and frustration. "But what clues? This room is bare!"

"On the contrary, Roosevelt. It has an interesting story to tell. Hargreave?"

"Go ahead, Holmes," nodded the young detective.

"The evidence indicates that the assassins who lurked in this room were prepared to use a rifle to be fired through this opened window.

Indeed, the weapon and the marksman were at the ready through the night. Observe the floor below the window. Notice the scratches in the paint, indicating that something was placed at the window as a steadying platform for the sniper and his weapon. Judging by these marks on the floor and on examining the legs of the bureau, I believe it is reasonable to state that the piece of furniture was moved for that purpose to this spot from its accustomed one against that wall. If you take the time to study the bureau, which the conspirators replaced, you will see that it had been moved and that someone or something rested upon it. There are distinct impressions in the dust atop the bureau, impressions that would be made by a man resting his arms upon it in just the position that a man would hold himself if he held a rifle in his hands. But, back to the floor by the window! Note the cigarette ashes! The ashes are of two varieties, indicating the presence of at least a pair of cigarette smokers in this room during the night."

"We are looking for two men, then," I nodded.

"Three, Roosevelt! Three!" exclaimed Holmes, turning away from the window toward the bed. "Observe on the floor at the edge of the bed there is a cigar band! And, I might point out, an expensive cigar! The man who patiently sat upon the edge of this bed and calmly smoked his expensive cigar was a man of some wealth. Probably, he is the man who has been supervising this dastardly scheme."

"Amazing, Holmes. What else does this room tell you?"

"That the men at the window wore brown boots; the man at the bed was wearing a black suit, possibly evening wear, with black shoes, of course; the man at the bed was at first highly agitated but settled down for his patient wait with his costly cigar."

"Incredible," I gasped.

Hargreave spoke up. "I now see the scuff marks at the window, made by brown boots."

"Exactly. Freshly made marks upon the baseboard."

"And the man in black at the bed?"

"Lint from his clothing on the coverlet. It is from an exquisitely woven fabric of the type found in evening wear."

"Therefore a man in evening clothes would wear black shoes!" I remarked.

"The faculty of deduction is certainly contagious, Roosevelt!" Holmes smiled, clapping me on the shoulder. "Congratulations! Are you able to tell me why I may state so positively that this well-dressed rascal at first was agitated?"

"Well," I said, thoughtfully studying the room for those little clues which Holmes so readily noticed, "while I see no physical evidence of it, I believe that were I here to command an attempt to murder a President I would be rather agitated."

"Bravo, Roosevelt. Of course, there *is* physical evidence to support your superbly stated surmise. Again, you must look at the floor. A definite trail of footprints in the dust from bed to wall and back, a pattern repeated over and over. The sure sign of a nervous man is a man whose footprints show that he was pacing. Yet we know he ultimately sat calmly on the bed for a smoke. We can deduce, therefore, that he began to realise that their plan to murder the President had gone awry, inasmuch as Mr Hayes did not put in the expected appearance at the expected time. Sitting down to ponder this turn of events, our well-dressed assassin left the room, at last. But the others seem to have remained on the chance that their scheme could succeed."

"Your timely intervention prevented that," I exclaimed.

"Yes, but we do not know who these men are or if they plan to strike again."

"These three men did not appear and disappear like ghosts," said Hargreave. "They are flesh and blood and, like us, they came into this hotel through the door. Therefore, someone may have seen them and from those persons we may be able to get descriptions and, possibly, names and addresses."

"The kind of investigation which is best done by a large force of trained men," said Holmes: "I assume you have in mind the sort of trusted investigators you need to pursue this angle of our problem, Hargreave?"

"I do. I'll choose men from the Broadway Squad."

"New York's finest," nodded Holmes.

"And what about you, Holmes?" I asked. "What is your next move?"

"It is about time I had an interview with the Sage of Gramercy Park, the Honorable Samuel Jones Tilden."

Eleven

๛

"What a tragic occurrence," commented Samuel J. Tilden as he admitted Sherlock Holmes and me into the ornately decorated parlour of his impressive house. "I was not here last night, as you may know, but on learning of the event I came in from my country estate in Yonkers immediately."

"Did you know that Tebbel, the man who was murdered, had been on his way to this very house at the time of his death?" asked Holmes. "I can see from your reaction that you did not know this!" he added.

"Indeed not! What an extraordinary thing!"

Tilden, who was by nature a nervous man given to awkward movements, stood by the fireplace and peered into the dark and cold hearth, his broad, intellectual brow knitted with worry. Tilden was unimpressive in physical appearance, but it had not been his physical personality that had made him an outstanding corporate lawyer, sagacious financier and successful political leader. It was the intellect behind that broad brow, those large blue eyes. A soft-spoken man, he would not have been a man one would have expected to succeed in politics where a forceful podium style is required.

"Something troubles you," observed Holmes, which seemed a superfluous remark in view of the fact that a man had been shot to death on Tilden's doorstep.

"I believe the man who was killed had attempted to communicate with me prior to last evening," Tilden said quietly.

"How did he try to communicate with you?" asked Holmes anxiously.

"There was a very peculiar letter delivered to my door two or three days ago by a messenger boy. I glanced at it only, because I was just leaving for 'Greystone.' That's the name of my Yonkers estate. Like so many requests for meetings and audiences, this letter asked to see me on a matter described as important. Well, I have long recognised that the word important has been corrupted through misuse. Unfortunately it is the lot of any wealthy man, but especially one in politics, to find himself confronted at every turn with favour seekers. I will tell you a secret! I have had built into the cellar of this house a tunnel that lets me escape out the back when someone is at the front whom I don't wish to see."

"Very enterprising," smiled Holmes. "Why do you believe that the message that came a few days ago was from the man who was murdered last night?"

"You said his name was Tebbel?"

"Yes."

"That was the name on the letter."

"Have you that letter?"

"In all probability," said Tilden, crossing the parlour to a pull-cord to summon a servant, to whom Tilden described the message in question. Yes, said the servant – an elderly black man, the message was with other similar ones in the library.

Fetching it, the servant handed it to Tilden, who agreed that it was the very letter. He passed it to Holmes.

"Tebbel's name, all right," muttered Holmes.

Peering over Holmes' shoulder, I was able to read the typewritten letter:

Dear Mr Tildin:

    I have to sea you on a matter of great importins.
    I have to sea you befor it is to late.

               Your ob'dnt servunt,
               N. Tebbel

"I can see why you dismissed this with such alacrity," stated Holmes.

"I am not a snob, sir, but I have had a great deal of experience with exactly this kind of importuning, and as I was in a hurry to leave my home on business and because the letter gave no particulars of what the matter was or when the man wished to see me, I had little choice but to lay it aside."

"Certainly, Mr Tilden. I meant no criticism," apologised Holmes. "Had you any previous indication that Tebbel was trying to see you?"

"Now that you mention it, just a day or so before this letter was brought, a roundsman had quite an altercation across the street with a fellow who had been loitering near the park. As you know, the charming park around which these homes stand is privately owned. Residents of this square have keys to the park, and because many of the residents are persons of prominence and wealth, the city police take pains to see that the peace and tranquility of our park and its environs are protected."

"Did you see the altercation?"

"No. My servant observed it and told me about it. I gave no further thought to it until now. Do you suppose that the loiterer was Tebbel?"

"It appears so," nodded Holmes. "May I take this letter with me?"

"It's of no use to me," shrugged Tilden. "However, in view of what I understand to be the circumstances of that unfortunate man's death – a common street assault – I am fascinated by your interest in the case and, quite naturally, I am now wondering why that man was so determined to visit me."

"I cannot give you the details now, sir, but the moment I am free to divulge the details of the case, I will share them with you, but only on condition that you tell no one else."

"Now you have truly stimulated my interest!" chuckled Tilden.

"Good day, then, sir. And thank you."

"I say, Roosevelt," said the Sage of Gramercy Park as Holmes and I turned to leave, "I understand that you are planning to marry in the autumn?"

"I am, sir."

"Do I know the young woman?"

"Her name is Alice Hathaway Lee."

"The Boston Lees?"

"The same."

"I do know her, and she is a charming young woman. My congratulations to you."

"Thank you, sir."

"And what about politics?"

"I am considering it."

"But you *must* run for something, Roosevelt. The political field needs bright young men such as you. Especially, politics needs men of integrity!"

"I am a Republican, of course," I reminded the illustrious old Democrat.

"I would say that Republicans particularly need men of integrity," Tilden joked.

While I would have been delighted to debate the strong points and weak points of Tilden's Democratic party, I observed a flaring impatience with this small talk in Holmes' eyes. We excused ourselves from the presence of that outstanding political figure. "What can that letter tell us?" I asked Holmes as we walked briskly across Gramercy Square in the direction of Twenty-second Street and Holmes' rooms.

"It is a rare opportunity," said Holmes excitedly, "because, as you plainly see, the letter was composed on a typewriter!"

"What of it? Those machines are everywhere."

"Yes, but we are dealing with Nigel Tebbel who was, given the awful condition of his spelling, an ignorant young man. Yet he had the use of a typewriter to compose this letter to Tilden! I have been making a study of the typewriter and its connection to crime, and this fortunate piece of evidence is likely to add a great deal to the monograph I expect to write on the topic, in addition to contributing to the solution of our current problem. Come in to my lodgings for a few minutes while I examine this letter beneath my glass."

"I fail to see how typewritten words will lead you to the conspirators," I remarked, peering over Holmes' shoulder.

"You are quite right, but by closely examining the characteristics of the machine which typed this letter I will, once we find the machine, conclusively prove that it was the one used by Tebbel. Having established that, I will have shown a connection between Tebbel and the person who owns the machine."

"And I now expect you to name that person!" I said in jest, turning away to find a comfortable chair.

"I cannot give you his name, Teddy," said Holmes as he half turned in his chair to peer across the clutter at me, "but I am reasonably certain it's Mr Well-dressed and that he will have some connection with a political club of some kind, for this conspiracy is the work of a political man, surely. That is why I feel so fortunate in having you at my side in this matter. You know politics. I don't. For example, where would a politically motivated Mr Well-dressed be likely to spend an evening out?"

"Easy," said I. "The Hoffman House Hotel, where we dined last evening, is a favourite for political men. If he is the sort to join a club and is a Republican, the Union League. If a Democrat..."

"I'm reasonably sure Mr Well-dressed is a Republican. Sorry, Teddy, if that offends you, but I am convinced this is a plot by a fanatical member of one of those party factions you so eloquently described for me."

"But why not a Democratic faction?" I asked, rising and not even trying to mask my displeasure at the thought that men of my own party would engage in such skulduggery.

"Why would Democrats want to murder a Republican President when the Vice-President who succeeds him would be a Republican as well? Besides, the Democrats have a chance to elect one of their own in November."

"I hope that does not occur," I stated emphatically.

"Always the partisan, Roosevelt?"

"I certainly do not fancy having another war hero in Washington."

"Mr Well-dressed is pursuing his deadly game," said Holmes, returning to the point, "out of personal pique against Hayes. That seems clear enough, for there is nothing to be gained politically by murdering a President who has been relegated to one term by the simple process of not having been nominated at the party's recent convention. Anyway, I have found that political assassinations which seem to have political motives on closer examination turn out to be the work of an individual driven by a personal animosity toward his victim, or, as in the case of John Wilkes Booth, the work of a man with an inflated sense of personal importance and a desire for notoriety. You see, I do not hold to the views of those who hold that all of history is a series of conspiracies.""Yet we have one before us," I pointed out.

"Yes, a conspiracy arranged by one foully motivated and wealthy individual who has hired thugs and misfits to even some score for him by murdering Hayes. The goal in this conspiracy is personal gratification, I believe. Not political advantage. I pray I am not wrong in this."

"As do I," I added.

"Listen! Someone is coming up the stairs, and if I am correct it is our colleague Hargreave. He's in a hurry, so he must have had some success."

Sure enough, a moment later, Hargreave burst excitedly into the room. "We've found him, Holmes! We've located the hack driver who picked up our friend in the evening wear!"

"Capital, Hargreave! Where is the hackie? I must question him minutely."

"Downstairs," said Hargreave, smiling.

"Bring him up, man!"

Twelve

M y name is Schulman," said the hack driver, a man of middle years with a shy, self-effacing manner and a nervous habit of holding his top hat by the brim and turning it in rapid revolutions as he spoke, "and I stable my horse Nell at a very reasonable establishment on West Street. I make it my habit to work during the daytime because I have a missus, a dear gal named Heidi, who doesn't care for me leaving her alone at night while I work the streets, although the best money is to be made at night, of course. But in consideration of her feelings, I work days, leaving my stable at the crack of dawn. I had just begun my day's work and was passing a certain hotel of the worst possible reputation when I was very surprised to see an unexpected customer hailing me in front of that hotel."

"What was unexpected about this customer?" asked Holmes, who stood quite still by the mantel of his sitting room, his grey eyes riveted on the nervous Schulman and his twirling topper.

"He was a gentleman, dressed to the hilt."

"Evening dress?" I asked.

"A very handsome cut of clothes. I used to work in the garment trade before I saved enough money to buy my hack, so I know a good cut of clothes, sir."

"Was there anything else you noticed about this fare?" asked Holmes, casually reaching for a briar and slowly stuffing it with shag.

"If you could be specific, sir?"

"His manner? Was he relaxed, hurried?"

"Oh, definitely hurried! He came out of that hotel as if the Devil himself were in pursuit!"

"Where did you take him?" asked Holmes.

"The Union League Club."

"A club with very strong political connections," I noted for Holmes' benefit.

"Yes," said Holmes. "The Club has recently moved into new quarters on Fifth Avenue at Thirty-ninth Street."

"A fine building it is, too," volunteered Schulman.

"Do you recall what this unusual passenger looked like?" I asked.

"Oh, he was a very impressive fellow and would not be easy to forget. He's a great, tall man and very huskily built. A lush moustache and very handsome muttonchop whiskers."

"You would recognise him again if you saw him, then," said Holmes, putting a match to his bowl and puffing clouds of pungent smoke.

"I'd know Mr Veil anywhere, sir," stated the hack driver with a decisive nod.

"Veil? You know this man's name?" asked Holmes, delightedly.

"That was the name spoken by the doorman at the Union League Club as he helped the gentleman from my cab," replied Schulman.

"Sir," smiled Sherlock Holmes, crossing the room while fishing from his pocket a bill, "you are an astonishing fellow and we are in your debt. I hope this will express adequately our appreciation."

"It will, sir!" smiled Schulman, taking a ten-dollar note Holmes offered.

"This is a matter in which Detective Hargreave may wish to speak with you again. You understand that?" asked Holmes.

"You want me as a witness, eh?" asked Schulman.

"It may not come to that," said Holmes, "but Hargreave will wish to know where to reach you."

"I'm always glad to cooperate with the authorities, sir."

"A remarkable man," said Holmes after the hack driver had left us in the company of Hargreave, who returned to Holmes' rooms. "I compliment you and your Broadway Squad for such quick and excellent police work, Hargreave. Now, shall we pay a call at the Union League Club?"

"Lest you think ill of the Union League Club, Holmes," I stated as we climbed into a four-wheeler, "I must tell you that no matter what evil deeds this fellow Veil may have done, the Club is an upright and exemplary institution! The finest men of New York are members and they are dedicated to performing civic duties unstintingly. The Union League has been instrumental in the organisation of the Metropolitan Museum of Art, among other notable works."

"I assure you, Roosevelt, I have nothing but the highest regard for the Union League Club. It has to be a fine organisation to count you as a member."

"I have not said that I am a member."

"No, but only a member would rise so passionately to defend a club which no one has come close to criticising," laughed Holmes.

"Do you happen to know Mr Veil?" asked Hargreave.

"The name is new to me" I replied.

"Well, he is certainly known at the Club to have been greeted by name by the doorman, so we should have no difficulty in locating him," said Holmes.

The Union League Club, an imposing structure on the northeast corner of Fifth and Thirty-ninth, was the work of the architects Peabody and Stearns with the interior designed by John LaFarge and Louis Tiffany. As our carriage drew up to the front of the building, a Negro doorman in elegant livery opened the door of our carriage and bowed a greeting. "Good day," said Holmes, stepping down to the sidewalk. "Do you know if Mr Veil is having luncheon at the Club today?"

"I don't believe so, sir," said the doorman as Hargreave and I left the carriage.

"Is he in the Club at this time?" I asked.

"No, sir," said the doorman. "Mr Veil left about twenty minutes ago."

"Do you know where he went?" asked Holmes urgently.

"He told his driver to take him to the Fifth Avenue Hotel, sir."

"Are we speaking of the same Mr Veil?" asked Holmes. "A tall man, heavily built, mustache, whiskers?"

"That's Mr Veil. Only one Mr Veil," smiled the doorman.

"Thank you," snapped Holmes, climbing back into the carriage. "Come, gentlemen," he said to Hargreave and me. "We were mistaken, apparently. We are dining with Mr Veil at the Fifth Avenue Hotel."

We arrived at the corner of Thirtieth Street in a few minutes to plunge into the noisy, bustling lobby. "I suggest that we have a look, first, in the Amen Corner," I stated as we pushed into the crowd. "I am quite familiar with this hotel and with the habits of the political men who frequent it. The Amen Corner is a small, lavish sitting room off this lobby at the end opposite us. The room has been so named because it was used by the Republican boss, Tom Platt, whose custom was to hold court there while seated in a rocking chair. A man such as Platt is forever surrounded by sycophants and yes-men, hence the name in recognition of the 'Amens' these toadies uttered at Platt's every word."

"Your colourful American politics becomes more colourful every passing second, Roosevelt, and if the eye of our hackie friend, Schulman, was not in error, I believe I see the tall form of Mr Veil in that very spot you suggested. I believe, Hargreave, that if you approach Mr Veil, whisper to him that you wish to speak with him on a police matter, and then bring him to that rather quiet little corner over there, we may soon learn if Veil is our man."

While Hargreave discreetly approached Veil, Holmes and I moved to the quiet corner Holmes had elected for our meeting and waited. Presently, Hargreave brought Veil to us, although the tall gentleman appeared to be quietly and with dignity protesting Hargreave's intrusion upon him at the Amen Corner. He was precisely as Schulman had described him – a giant of a man, impeccable in his dress, and of a deportment that approached the imperious.

"This is most extraordinary," he exclaimed as Hargreave presented him to Sherlock Holmes and me. "Further, it is very embarrassing. The idea! Being spirited away from my friends by a policeman!"

"Are you a guest of this hotel?" asked Holmes.

"I am," replied Veil angrily. "I have a suite."

"Then I suggest we adjourn to your suite where we may conduct our business more discreetly?"

"I shall not move from this spot until you explain this outrageous behavior."

"Very well," said Holmes. "It is a case of murder. A case in which some evidence quite clearly points to you. On the chance that there has been some mistake—"

"There certainly has been!"

"—We merely wish to offer you the opportunity to make explanations."

"Very well. Come then, to my suite."

The commodious accommodations were on the fifth floor of the hotel overlooking busy Broadway. The sitting room appeared to have been furnished with extra chairs and couches, a fact which Holmes recognised immediately. "You seem to have had a number of business meetings in recent days, Mr Veil."

"And why not? The Republican National Committee has been convening in this very hotel in order to prepare for the campaign. I am quite a prominent personage in the Republican party, sir, as your friend, the young Mr Roosevelt should know."

"I have been engaged in my studies, Mr Veil, and have not kept up with the daily business of the Republican party," I explained. "Are you leased with the choice of Garfield?"

"I was won over by the compromise which put Arthur on the ticket."

"Ah, you are a Stalwart," I said with a smile.

"I am and proud of it."

Sherlock Holmes, who had taken advantage of my distraction of Veil to quickly look around Veil's parlor, discovered a small writing table near a window. "I see that you have a typewriting machine," he announced.

"And what, may I ask, is so unusual about my having a typewriting machine?" asked Veil, his face flushing red with anger.

"I am fascinated by them," said Holmes, pulling out the chair and seating himself before the machine. Taking a sheet of paper and rolling it into the typewriter, he added, "Did you know that typewriting machines are quite distinctive and that each impression made by them is entirely different from another?"

"Very interesting," said Veil impatiently.

"Yes, isn't it?" said Holmes, pecking at the keyboard of the machine. Quite suddenly, his fingers flew over the keys with amazing speed, causing a rattling, chattering noise, like the rapid fire of rifles. Just as suddenly, he stopped, tore the paper from the machine, and crossed the room with it. "Have a look at the typewritten words on this paper," he said. Then, reaching into his inside pocket, he withdrew what I immediately recognised as the letter which Tebbel had sent to Samuel J. Tilden. "Compare what I have just typewritten with the printing on this letter."

"What of it?" snapped Veil.

"Surely you can see that this letter from N. Tebbel was written on the very machine that produced the verbatim copy of Tebbel's letter which I just produced?"

Pushing aside the letters in Holmes' hands, Veil laughed, "The words are the same nothing more."

"Ah, but you are quite wrong, sir. Observe the letter *e*, which is slightly askew. The letter *a* in the words 'have,' 'sea,' 'a,' 'great,' 'late,' and 'Dear' in the salutation. See how the 'a' is clogged with ink. There are at least a dozen other identical characteristics to be found in these letters, proving conclusively that they were made on the same machine." Holmes passed the letters to Hargreave. "Further, the incontrovertible fact that Tebbel made his letter on this very typewriter is proof that Tebbel was in this room!"

"Hundreds of persons have been in this room!" scoffed Veil. "As you can see, I have had numerous meetings here during the course of the conferences associated with the National Committee."

"Do you know Tebbel?" asked Hargreave, glancing up from the pair of typewritten letters.

"I know a great many people, sir," sighed Veil, sinking heavily into corner of a massive brocaded couch. "I may even have known this man Tebbel."

"Shall we bring Tebbel here?" asked Holmes.

This statement startled me, for Tebbel, of course, was dead, but I immediately saw that Holmes was playing a trick – one which had its effect on Veil, who turned white as a ghost. The shock, surprise, and terror in Veil's face convinced me that he was our man and quite likely had ordered Tebbel's murder. (Being a policeman, Hargreave exhibited no expression of surprise at Holmes' statement.)

"Once again, I must protest this very peculiar line of questioning," muttered Veil, recovering slightly from his momentary shock.

"Make matters easy on yourself, Mr Veil," suggested Hargreave. "We know what you have been up to."

Regaining his imperious and offended tone, Veil stormed, "I have no idea what you are talking about!"

"I am talking about your presence in a room in a hotel, quite different from this one, through the night, and your sinister purpose in being there," said Hargreave, his voice rising angrily.

"I have been in no hotel but this one! I spent the entire night in these rooms!"

"Protest if you will," said Holmes quietly, "but we have a witness who places you at an address on West Street, and I am certain that physical evidence will bear out the testimony of the witness."

"I have no idea what you are getting at, but I shall certainly see that my lawyer brings suit against you, sir, whoever you are!"

"Come now," said Holmes, "let's not beat around the bush, to borrow one of your American idioms. We know you were at the address on West Street and we know your purpose. We can prove your connection with Nigel Tebbel. I believe you gave the order for his murder! Though you may deny all of these allegations, I assure you that we have the proof! It will go easier for you if you admit it and tell us who your accomplices are and where they may be found."

"Speak up, man," added Hargreave, unmistakably the policeman.

Thirteen

∾

Augustus Tiberius Gaius Nero Veil mopped his broad brow with a delicately lacy handkerchief and sipped frequently from a tall glass of iced water as he peered across his opulent sitting room at Sherlock Holmes, who presented a leisurely, almost lackadaisical, posture as he half reclined in a wingback chair – pointy chin in cupped palm, head tilted to the side, long legs crossed at the knees – as if he were listening to music instead of the despicable confession which Veil proceeded to make.

"You are on to me, I can see that," Veil had stated resignedly at the beginning of his discourse, "so I will relate to you the entire matter, my role in it, and those who joined me in the enterprise, which certainly would have succeeded had not Tebbel gotten cold feet at the most critical moment. I was surprised at him, because I thought Tebbel above all others would do anything for money. He was a dope fiend, you see."

"Cocaine," Holmes noted.

"You know even that!"

"Begin at the beginning, please."

"I have been devoted to the Republican party since the very day I reached my majority. I cast my first vote for Lincoln in 1860 and worked hard for his victory. My diligent work was duly noted by leaders of our party here in New York, and it has been my honour to serve the party in numerous capacities since that time. Earlier, I had been introduced to the political world by my father, who took me with him to the first Republican state convention in New York at Saratoga, after which I was an observer of the campaign for Fremont in 1856. I enjoyed the thrill of politics even then, you see. It was at the 1856 convention that I first met Chet Arthur. Although Chet was a few years older than I, we became friends and it has been my privilege to serve him in numerous capacities since that time. I worked side by side with him in the campaign for the re-election of Governor Edwin Morgan, and when Chet was rewarded for his efforts with the rank of brigadier general, performing duties in the war connected with supplying New York volunteers, I served him as an aide. I continued in that capacity until Chet returned to private life in 1863. A Democrat had been elected governor that year!

"I remained as active in the Republican ranks as did Arthur. Chet was soon regarded as second only to Senator Conkling in power and influence in the party. At that time, I had the privilege, again, of being of service to Chet, although by then I was a prominent businessman, of course, so Chet and I were more on an equal footing than previously. I became a member of Chet's political club, working for Grant in '68. When Grant appointed Chet to the post of Collector of the Port of New York, I was invited to assist him in the dispensing of patronage. Then, last year, Hayes — that despicable cur! — dismissed Chet from the job!"

"And you?" asked Holmes quietly.

"Naturally, I resigned in protest."

"Proceed, please."

"I then determined to remove the despot, even as that noble Roman, Brutus, had removed the despotic Julius Caesar."

"Assassin!" I muttered angrily, thumping my clenched fist upon the arm of my chair.

With only a glance in my direction, Veil went on, "I made up my mind to avenge Hayes' affront to Arthur and the Stalwarts and to perform a genuine service to my country. The removal of a tyrant is an act of patriotism! I was fortunate in coming across a man who shared my view and who had, in fact, made an unsuccessful attempt to achieve the same end while Hayes was in Columbus, Ohio, last month. No one found out about this attempt upon the President at the time. Rather, it was hidden by the publication of reports of a rumour that the President had collapsed of an illness on a Columbus street. In fact, a shot had been fired. The President escaped injury only because a bystander had seen a suspicious movement a moment before the shot was fired and threw the President to the ground. It was by chance that I ran into the man who had fired the shot a few days ago. He had had a few too many drinks and was declaiming loudly in the bar downstairs about what he thought of Hayes and what ought to be done about him. I drew the man aside and eventually I learned of his previous attack upon the President. Here, I decided, was my man!"

"His name?" asked Holmes without stirring from his slouch.

"Rickards."

"Where is he now?" asked Hargreave.

"I have no idea, although we are to meet this evening."

"Where?"

"The Silver Dollar Bar in the Gilsey Hotel."

"And his accomplice?" asked Holmes.

"I have mentioned no accomplice," said Veil.

"But there is one," snapped Holmes, coming upright in his chair.

"Initials of C. G."

"I know him only by the name Charles," signed Veil, now utterly defeated and overwhelmed by his circumstances.

"Will Charles be with Rickards at the Silver Dollar?" asked Hargreave.

"They have become inseparable."

"It is a peculiarity of persons involved in murderous conspiracies to develop a distinct aversion to leaving their fellow conspirators alone," stated Holmes. "Which of these cutthroats murdered Tebbel?"

"I have no idea. I didn't ask."

"Why was Tebbel killed?" I asked.

"As I stated, cold feet."

"Was it that? Or did he at last recoil at the prospect of assassination?" I exclaimed.

"Whatever his motive," shrugged Veil, "he left a meeting with Rickards and Charles at that same hotel on West Street with the purpose of going to someone in authority to abort our mission. I knew nothing of this until I joined Charles and Rickards at the hotel to await the President's return from Hoboken. On my arrival, I was told that it had been necessary to eliminate Tebbel. I asked no questions. We waited all night for Hayes to come back to Manhattan. He didn't. I presume you gentlemen had something to do with that unexpected development."

"Yes," nodded Holmes. "It was Rickards who recruited Charles and Tebbel?"

"Quite so," nodded Veil.

"Augustus Tiberius Gaius Nero Veil," announced Will Hargreave, "I arrest you as an accomplice-after-the-fact to the murder of Nigel Tebbel and for conspiracy to assassinate the President of the United States."

So saying, Hargreave produced a pair of handcuffs and snapped them upon Veil's wrists.

"For the moment," suggested Holmes, "hold him on the accomplice-to-murder charge, but give out no news of this arrest until we have apprehended Rickards and Charles. Even then it may not be wise to press a charge of a conspiracy against the President. Take him away, Hargreave! Roosevelt and I will be at my lodgings awaiting your return."

"What now, Holmes?" I asked as Hargreave conducted Veil from the room.

"Now we must bide our time until the appointed hour when Veil was to meet his two companions. We, of course, shall take his place at that meeting and, so, put an end to this business once and for all."

"I was amazed at your deportment while Veil told his infamous tale," I remarked as we left the hotel.

"How should I have conducted myself, Roosevelt?" he asked, signaling the doorman to fetch us a hackney.

"Anger! Surprise!"

"Anger? Yes, I felt a twinge of that. Assassination is an especially abhorrent crime. But surprise? Not a bit of it. I found nothing surprising in Veil's dissertation. Besides, to be surprised is to evidence a flawed character for a man who is engaged in my business. It is a flaw that could be fatal. Now, we have a cab and a few hours to while away, so may I suggest luncheon at my rooms? My landlady has taken a fancy to me and worries that I don't eat properly and so has broken her own rule against her boarders taking meals in the rooms. Then, at six, we'll rendezvous with Rickards and Charles and arrest them. As I promised you, I will have ample time to present myself at the Union Square Theatre for tonight's performance of *Twelfth Night*."

The meal served by the landlady, a charming Italian woman who clearly cared more for Holmes than he detected, was superb, and it was followed by the most amazing demonstration of musical ability which I have ever witnessed in an amateur, as Holmes rendered what

I must honestly call a virtuoso performance on a violin which he produced from a corner of his rooms.

This delightful afternoon ended on an alarming note, however, with the arrival of Hargreave.

"Veil is dead!" he announced, breathlessly.

"Dead? How?" exclaimed Holmes, bolting from his chair.

"By his own hand, Hanged himself in his cell at Mulberry Street!"

"Damn him," cried Holmes. "What a fool! Suicide! No man has the right to take his own life! Did he leave a note?"

"No."

"Just as well."

"Where does this leave us?" I asked.

"Our situation is unchanged. Two of these conspirators are dead — Tebbel and Veil. We will arrest the others — Rickards and Charles. That will close this problem."

Fourteen

ℰ♪

Wilson Hargreave waited inconspicuously in the vestibule of a
house across Broadway from the Gilsey Hotel as Holmes and I
arrived by carriage. Stepping down, I glanced at the ornate cast-iron
facade of the eight-storey hotel, one of the most notable architectural
achievements in New York. The Silver Dollar Bar encompassed much of
the ground floor, but the hour was early and there was little traffic into
and out of the popular gathering spot. Will greeted us somberly as we
entered the vestibule to join him in waiting for the arrival of our quarry.

I had become even more admiring of Will Hargreave in the short span
of our mutual adventure, my admiration grounded primarily in his
willingness to observe and learn from the extraordinary techniques of our
young English detective, but by no means had Will neglected his own
duties, as he made evident upon our arrival. "The very best men from the
Broadway Squad are inside the Silver Dollar," he announced proudly with
a nod toward the establishment. "And I've placed a man at each corner.
All have been given the descriptions of Charles and Rickards which you
obtained from Griggs. If the fellow was accurate in his observations, we'll

have no trouble spotting that unlikely pair of scoundrels."

"Your men are armed?" asked Holmes.

"They are," said Hargreave with an emphatic nod. "And you?"

"I have my revolver and Roosevelt has his," said Holmes.

"Well," chuckled Will, "if Teddy's armed, we have nothing to fear. He's a crack shot."

"However, I have never shot at a *man*," I pointed out.

"Now," sighed Holmes, slouching against a wall and peering through the window at the hotel, "we must pay the price of being detectives. We must wait."

"Mr Hayes is on his way back to the capital," said Hargreave, breaking a silence that had settled upon us during our waiting. "He goes home to the White House in your debt, sir."

"That I have been of service is enough," shrugged Holmes.

"Had it not been for you, Holmes," I chimed in, "a great tragedy would have occurred, surely. You should not lightly dismiss your work in this case. I will never forget how you saw that a seemingly ordinary street murder masked a conspiracy with assassination as its goal."

"I expect that when a man has special knowledge and special powers like my own, it makes him look for a complex explanation when a simpler one is at hand."

"I intend to see that official notice is taken of your work in this case," stated Hargreave.

With a frown, Holmes replied, "No. I am not interested in accolades or rewards."

"Then I will give you something as a personal tribute," insisted Hargreave.

"A personal memento will be fine," said Holmes. "I shall look forward to it. Ah, what is that across the way?"

As we three turned to look toward the hotel, a carriage drew to the curb and two men stepped out, but the passengers were obscured for a long, painfully breathless moment until the carriage drew away, revealing the backs of two men who in no way approached the descriptions of Rickards and Charles.

"We must wait a little while longer," sighed Holmes, leaning against the wall once more.

"Perhaps they caught wind of what has happened and won't come," I suggested glumly.

"There is no way they could know of Veil's fate," replied Hargreave. "Not a word of it has reached the newspapers!"

"I believe our men will be here," added Holmes, "sooner or later." Coming up straight again, his cold eyes peering toward the hotel, he added, "And *sooner* rather than later!"

"It's Rickards, all right," whispered Hargreave excitedly. "Bigger than I'd expected but there's no missing that mop of red hair."

"No mistaking the mousy Charles either," I pointed out. As the immense Rickards swaggered toward the Gilsey Hotel, the smaller, pale, thin Charles walked rapidly at his side, trying to keep up with the bigger man's pace. Rickards wore the clothing of a longshoreman. Charles was in a black suit and slouched hat that seemed to me to be in perfect accord with his villainous character. The two were gesturing wildly.

"Our quarry appear to be having an argument," said Holmes.

"Shall we move in?" asked Hargreave.

With the words, my hand went into my pocket to find the comforting presence of my revolver.

"Let them come closer," said Holmes, laying a restraining hand upon Will's shoulder. "We don't want to alert them just yet."

In a few moments, Rickards and Charles were near to the entrance of the Silver Dollar. Their voices carried clearly across the street. Angrily, Charles was saying, "It's your fault that things have gotten out of hand. If you'd've taken care of Tebbel sooner, we'd have succeeded."

"Now we know who murdered Tebbel, eh?" whispered Holmes.

Rickards's reply to Charles was lost in the clopping of a horse's hooves and the rattle of a passing carriage, but Holmes and I could not help but hear Hargreave's choked gasp as he had his first close look at the two men across Broadway. "I know that little fellow! That is, I have seen him from time to time. He's a very disreputable hanger-on who has been haunting the Fifth Avenue Hotel and bothering the political men who do business there."

"Where he undoubtedly met Veil," I suggested.

"Yes," said Holmes.

"He might recognise me," warned Hargreave.

"He's seen you?" Holmes asked.

Will shrugged. "I don't know, but if I saw him it seems reasonable to assume—"

"Um," muttered Holmes. "We'll have to move quickly, then. I suggest we cross the street and arrest these men right now."

We left the vestibule and hurried down a flight of steps. Neither Rickards nor Charles noticed us. Indeed, they took no notice until they were about to push open the door of the Silver Dollar. Then the sound of our running alarmed them. They stopped, turned, saw us, and bolted in the direction from which they had come.

"Signal your man at the corner, Hargreave!" shouted Holmes, but no signal was needed. The policeman at the corner, deceptively attired in evening clothes, was already moving toward Rickards and Charles.

"Halt! Police!" cried Hargreave.

To no avail.

I whipped my revolver from my pocket, ready to fire.

"No, Teddy!" cried Holmes, knocking my arm down. It was a wise intervention. Had I fired, I could have struck the policeman who bounded in front of Rickards and Charles in an effort to block their path. Unfortunately, the daring and brave young member of the Broadway Squad proved no match for the massive Rickards and the wiry Charles and was thrown hard to the street. The culprits resumed their desperate bid to escape.

I fired one shot after them but missed.

Although Holmes, Hargreave, and I were running hard and closing the distance between us and the culprits, they had reached the corner, dashed into the street, and forced a passing hack to a halt. The burly Rickards leaped into the hack and shoved the hackie off his perch into the street. Charles scampered into the back of the hack like a ferret scrambling into its lair. The horse, at the crack of the whip in Rickards' hand, sprang forward, and the hack clattered south on Broadway.

"Damn!" cried Holmes.

Fifteen

With upraised arms and brandishing his badge, Hargreave dashed into Broadway to commandeer a passing carriage. "Stop! Police! We must have this coach!" Too startled and frightened to do anything but comply, the coach's occupants meekly climbed down and we scrambled into it, Hargreave leaping to the driver's box and seizing the reins.

"Ha!" cried Holmes, nostrils flaring, eyes ablaze with excitement. "We shall have these criminals, I promise you!"

Away, we flew down Broadway, Hargreave whipping the horse to greater exertion and our carriage to faster speeds while I held on for dear life, bounced and tossed upon the seat. Holmes stood, face in the wind, jaw firmly set with cold determination.

Ahead of us by several blocks clattered the pirated coach carrying Rickards and Charles, the hack bouncing and careering dangerously through screaming, scattering pedestrians who had found themselves haplessly in the path of the coach and its desperately mad passengers.

"Faster, Hargreave! Faster!" cried Holmes, bony hands clenching the back of the driver's seat.

"Sit down, Holmes!" I implored, tugging at his coattail. "You'll fall out!"

"We'll get them, Teddy! We'll get them!" he cried. "Or we'll die in the effort."

Hargreave proved an expert driver, keeping our pursuing carriage on a straight line with the object of our chase. Helped by the fact that their dangerous race down Broadway had cleared a way for us, we gained steadily.

"They're turning!" shouted Hargreave.

"Don't lose them!" shouted Holmes.

Holding tight, I managed to rise from my seat to watch Rickards wheel his stolen hack sharply to the east. In a moment, we had made the same turn, coming near to turning over, but soon we found a steady keel, plunging dangerously, recklessly along usually quiet, tree-lined Twenty-third Street. Here, too, frightened people ran for their lives as the speeding carriages suddenly bore down upon them. We raced past the City College of New York's building at the corner of Lexington and Twenty-third, only two blocks from the spot where the murder of Nigel Tebbel had launched us on our amazing course only a few hours earlier.

Rickards and Charles turned south on Third Avenue.

Hargreave maneuvered the turn and closed the distance a bit more.

"The horse cannot keep up this pace!" I warned.

Holmes appeared not to hear my words.

Mercifully, the avenue emptied before us as terrified citizens scurried to the safety of sidewalks only to gape in amazement and anger as the racing carriages rattled head-long past them. We crossed over to The Bowery and then into the streets of The Five Points while ahead of us loomed the stolidly impressive towers of the unfinished bridge to Brooklyn.

"Your revolver, Roosevelt!" cried Holmes. "Use it now!"

Leaping to my feet and trying to steady my stance, I levelled my arm and sighted down the barrel of the weapon. Holmes braced his body against mine to help steady me. I fired twice, missing twice.

"Damn!" groaned Holmes, bringing out his pistol and firing with equally futile results.

"It's useless, Holmes, at this speed!"

"Close it up, Hargreave!" Holmes demanded.

My glance at the frothing, straining horse pulling our carriage was enough to tell me that we could not maintain this breakneck pace much longer. We had raced wildly for blocks. It was a wonder the animal had not dropped dead long ago!

"Ho!" Holmes laughed triumphantly. "Look! They've overturned!"

Sure enough! A chuckhole became their undoing, splitting a wheel and flipping the hackney into a spin and onto its side, their pitiful horse brought to its knees while the villains in the coach were plummeted to the street.

"Stop, Hargreave!" roared Holmes.

Even before we had come to a halt, Holmes leaped out of the coach to dash toward the fallen quarry. I leaped after him and Hargreave behind me. Rickards and Charles lay dazed in a gutter, but not for long.

"Watch out!" warned Holmes, throwing himself to the street.

Luckily, I saw what Holmes had seen – Rickards lifting himself onto an elbow to level a pistol at us. Dropping to the street and rolling against a curbstone, I heard the report of the weapon. It seemed to be the loudest noise I had ever heard! Yet it was lost immediately in the far more terrifying cry of pain from Hargreave. "I'm hit!" Looking back, I saw Will clutch his left shoulder. I scampered on all fours toward him as two other shots rang out.

"Will! Will! Are you badly hit?"

"The shoulder! Damn! It hurts like hell!"

"I'll get help!"

"No! Give Holmes a hand! Look!"

Sherlock Holmes was up to his feet again and chasing Rickards and Charles, who sprinted madly ahead of him. "I can't leave you hurt, Will," I protested.

"God damn it, Teddy! We can't let the scoundrels escape!"

By this time, Holmes was two blocks distant and the criminals a block ahead of him. When I closed most of that distance between them and me we had reached the approaches to the Manhattan side of the bridge that would soon be a highway across the East River to Brooklyn and Long Island. As I could not chance using my revolver because I might hit Holmes, there was nothing to do but run as fast as I could and, with Holmes, grapple with the two men who, now, had become the objects of the most intense hatred I had ever known. They had shot my friend Will Hargreave and that, I felt at that moment, was a far greater crime than their plot to murder our President or their dastardly murder of Nigel Tebbel! Dashing up the long slope of the bridge, I realised that my interest in this affair was now the basest motive in the entire human experience – revenge. Revenge for wounding my friend Will!

Then, with a flying tackle, Holmes – amazingly so for such a spare young man–brought down Rickards.

And I pounced upon the smaller man.

A vicious, cunning, skillful fighter and wrestler, Charles gave no quarter as we tangled, seizing each other around the middle and falling onto the planking of the floor of the bridge. Even though we were gasping, grunting, and breathing hard as we struggled, I heard the rush of East River waters far below us. Tenacious and shrewd, the wiry Charles clung to me, perhaps sensing that he would be in serious peril if I were free to use my fists.

Then, frantically, I suddenly heard Holmes crying to me. "Roosevelt! Teddy! Teddy!"

The horror of what I saw as I looked in the direction of that anguished cry can not be adequately put into words. The gargantuan Rickards had gotten the best of the young Englishman and was handling him as if he were a mere sapling which he was determined to break in two. Huge, thick hands throttled Holmes' throat. Worse, Holmes was backed against a guardrail, his head, shoulders, and the upper portion of his torso thrust precariously backward over the brink. With sickening horror, I saw that he was a hairbreadth away from being flung into the black, swirling waters far, far below.

I sprang to help.

With all the strength I could muster, I lunged against the hulking Rickards and the impact was enough to shake his grip on Holmes's throat. Turning away, the huge, red-haired abomination who had shot my friend Will and very nearly killed Holmes taunted me with a hateful grin. "I get *you*, now!" he boasted.

"If you are going to hit a man put him to sleep!"

The words were my father's − so clear in my head that I would have sworn he was standing beside me.

My right came up from my side in a long, wide, graceful but vicious arc.

When my fist struck flesh, I felt nose cartilage give way, as Will's had done years earlier in my boyhood boxing gym.

Rickards's hairy red face spattered with blood.

Roaring in pain, he stumbled blindly backward, faltered, crashed against and through the wooden railing where Holmes had dangled so precariously, and went over the side of the bridge. Oddly, he uttered no cry as he disappeared into the deep, rapidly flowing black waters below. He sank immediately and never came up.

Dazed, I stared down at the river until I felt someone shaking my shoulders. Regaining my senses, I turned and looked into the face of Sherlock Holmes. "Are you all right, Teddy?"

"Yes."

"You saved my life, old friend. I could have been down there."

Suddenly, I remembered Charles and turned to look for him.

"He's gone," sighed Holmes, nodding toward a distant figure in black scurrying over the dangerous length of the incomplete bridge. "He'll be in Brooklyn in a few minutes."

"We can't let him get away," I cried.

"I'm afraid he already has, Teddy."

Sixteen

When I again found my friend Holmes in his rooms on East Twenty-second Street, the cluttered sitting room was blue with smoke from his calabash pipe, as if he were deliberately creating a simulation of the famous London fog. He peered at me through this haze with cocked head and arched brows, "Ah, Roosevelt, come in. Is it morning already?"

"You've been up all night? Not fretting about the escape of Charles, I hope? I'm sure Hargreave will locate and arrest him."

"Perhaps," said Holmes.

"Be content, Holmes," I said cheerily.

"I am content only when I have a problem to work on, and at the moment I have none. I live only when the game's afoot."

"Well, you are to be congratulated on the successful termination of this business. The President is safely back at the Executive Mansion."

Holmes gave me a rare, quick smile. "You were an invaluable help to me."

"I did little."

"But you were there at my side, a trusty companion. I am grateful, and Hargreave also appreciates your assistance."

"That young man has taken a liking to you *and* your methods."

"He's told me as much. In fact, he offered me a job with the New York police."

"A bully idea!"

"Hargreave was around bright and early this morning. Not even a bullet wound can keep that fellow out of service."

"I saw him last evening," I said, "He'll mend perfectly."

"A brave man, and now he'll have a scar to boast about. And you, my friend, were not lacking in bravery either."

"I confess it was anger that motivated me to do what I did. Bravery had little to do with it."

"Well, bravery is usually the offspring of anger, isn't it?"

"I feel as if I have just put down a thrilling work of fiction. It is almost impossible to believe that what we have experienced really happened."

Holmes smiled. "Teddy, if we could make a magic flying tour of this magnificent city and magically see through the walls and rooftops of its houses, fiction would seem stale and unprofitable in the face of the queer things which are going on, the coincidences, the plans that are being made, the cross purposes, the chain of events leading to the most incredible results. There is nothing quite like life to be found in fiction, Roosevelt."

"Are you inured to life and yet so young?"

"Not at all. I am far from being inured. True, one could despair of life when confronting the likes of Veil or Rickards or the elusive Charles, but on the other hand, there are good men like Griggs. And Schulman, the hack driver with the alert senses! And the brave Hargreave! Not to mention a man named Theodore Roosevelt, who — what did Hargreave say of you? — walks quietly but carries a big fist!"

"Let's not forget a man named Holmes?"

Holmes crossed the room and scooped up a sheaf of newspapers lying at the foot of his chair. "Have you seen today's *Times?*"

"I have not," I said. "An account of the Gramercy Park affair?"

"The briefest account of Tebbel's murder. Nothing more, happily, of a case that is best left untold, but the *Times* in this number also has an article that has, I confess, stirred an emotion in me that I have long been battling to keep under control."

"Indeed? An article on what subject?"

Holmes handed me the newspaper and managed a wan smile before slumping again into his chair and lifting his calabash to his mouth. "See for yourself."

I could only chuckle with amusement at the title of the article: "Phases of London Life."

"It amuses you that a man of my years and sophistication is touched with homesickness by a mere newspaper article?"

"Of course it amuses me, but not at your expense. I was reminded of my own feelings of longing for more familiar streets and scenes when I first went to Cambridge. I found myself torn between a desire to read every New York newspaper I could find and a certain knowledge that the mere possession of a New York paper would tug at my heart strings."

"Home is where the heart is," said Holmes, puffing hard and adding to the density of the fog that swirled around us.

"Boats leave almost daily for England," I observed, tossing aside the newspaper and settling comfortably in a chair near his.

Holmes nodded. "Yes, but I am committed to completing the tour with Sasanoff. We go directly to Baltimore. It will be some time before I see London again."

"And some time before you leave it again?"

The detective smiled. "She is the queen of cities. There is so much work to do there. But what of Theodore Roosevelt?"

"I am off to the West. A long-awaited journey with my brother. When I return, I will take up the study of law and then…"

"Politics?"

I smiled. "I'm going to give it a try."

"And not long from now, I will find myself listening to my brother Mycroft, who keeps track of political news for me, regaling me with tales of the successes of Mr Roosevelt until, I am certain, that news will originate from Washington, D.C."

"It's an established American promise – that any man may aspire to become President of the United States," I boasted.

"Yes, Teddy! You have found precisely the word to sum up the greatness of your country. Promise! What promise there is in this land! Things happen in this country that could not happen anywhere else in the world. No, not even in my beloved England. There is an optimistic zest for tomorrow in every aspect of American life that is unlike that in any other country in the world. The new century that is so rapidly approaching is going to see the emergence of this rough, raw-boned, vital country into a colossus. The nineteenth has been the century of the English. The twentieth will belong to the United States of America. Men like you will see to it."

"A bright future, indeed."

"What have you planned for today?" he asked.

"Nothing important, really."

"Excellent! Then you are free to accompany me across the Hudson River? There is a fellow in New Jersey whom I wish to visit. Like you, he has been a correspondent of mine over the past few years. He's a fellow scientist. Perhaps you've heard of him? Thomas Edison?"

"The name sounds familiar."

"An amazing chap," said Holmes, slipping into his jacket crossing the room, and opening the door. "He is at work in his laboratory in a place called Menlo Park, and he is tinkering with inventions that will amaze you, utterly amaze you, the latest of which is an electric lamp. Three years ago he devised a phonograph, or speaking machine, and it is that device that I am going to Menlo Park to see demonstrated."

"A speaking machine. Yes, I recall an item about its patenting."

"Yes," said Holmes as we hurried down the stairs toward the street. "I foresee innumerable uses for such a device in the fight against crime. Think of it, Roosevelt! A machine capable of recording the human voice and reproducing it at will. Think of the implications in terms of gathering evidence, of transcribing conversations covertly, of having the recorded words – in their actual voices – of conspirators and criminals. Think of the advantage to law enforcement!"

We were quickly onto the street and signaling for a cab to take us to the ferry landing. Thence, across the broad Hudson to New Jersey, and as we travelled, the subdued and homesick fellow I had found in Holmes' rooms vanished. Beside me in the hansom was the quick, bright, animated Sherlock Holmes, who had deduced that a seemingly common street crime was part of a larger and more sinister conspiracy. His efforts had thwarted it, leaving nothing unanswered except for the identity of the elusive Charles, that furtive fellow who had escaped us.

While the excited Holmes, who was looking forward to meeting Mr Edison, sat beside me, he made no mention of any emotion he may have been experiencing – disappointment, surely, and frustration – at having failed to apprehend Charles. Nor did he evidence any outward sign that he would continue ruminating upon that one loose end in the puzzle.

His mind was to the future – to what he would learn in the laboratory of the amazing Mr Edison of Menlo Park.

Holmes was quiet until we were on the New Jersey side of the Hudson, but, as we settled into a railway coach for the trip to Menlo Park, he turned to me with a smile of pure excited anticipation to say, "I have been promised in my previous correspondence with Edison a personal demonstration of his phonograph. I have not decided whether I shall record a few lines from *Twelfth Night* or simply speak as myself. What do you suggest?"

"In the course of history there have been and will be many Malvolios, but Sherlock Holmes is, I deduce, one of a kind!"

Afterword

There are few instances of a failure by Sherlock Holmes, although there are tantalising allusions to them in Watson's writings.

Because Holmes thwarted a conspiracy to assassinate Rutherford B. Hayes it may seem unfair to say that Holmes failed in "The Adventure of the Stalwart Companions." Yet he did. He failed to capture the central figure in the case, that enigmatic, wily, furtive fellow named Charles.

While I do not have any evidence to show that Holmes eventually discovered who Charles was, it seems likely he did, perhaps through a chance remark by Holmes' brother Mycroft, on July 2, 1881 – one year after the murder of Nigel Tebbel at Gramercy Park. I imagine Holmes' discovery regarding Charles as follows.

Mycroft Holmes, a man whose giant body seemed designed by nature to accommodate his giant intellect, came into his brother's rooms without knocking, an irritating custom all his life. "Have you recovered the Duke's missing letters?" he asked.

Sherlock Holmes registered a passing surprise, then smiled. "Of course! It had to be *you* who whispered my name in the Duke's ear as the one person who could retrieve the compromising letters!"

"To be precise," said Mycroft, settling heavily into a chair, "I whispered your name to the 'other woman' and *she* whispered your name to the Duke!"

"I shall have the letters in my possession at midnight."

"The Duke will be relieved."

"And grateful, I hope, for my bill will be reflective of the difficulty I have had in the case. And why are you going to the Foreign Office at this late hour?"

Mycroft smiled, recognising himself all the little clues about his appearance and deportment that had led his brother to deduce that he was, indeed, going to call upon the Foreign Minister. "I have been asked to give my assessment of the possible effects on the Empire of the assassination of the American President."

"What?" gasped Sherlock Holmes, bolting away from his desk and striding to his brother's chair. "President Garfield has been murdered?"

"He is mortally wounded. Confidentially, he will not survive very long. I thought you would have heard about this."

"I have not left these rooms in two days' time."

"President Garfield was boarding a train at Washington's Baltimore and Potomac railway station for a journey to attend the twenty-fifth reunion of his class at Williams College. A mentally deranged man came out of the crowd and shot the President pointblank, two shots. One hit Garfield in the arm. The other, the mortally wounding one, struck him in the back. A dastardly deed."

"And the assassin?"

"As I said, a mentally deranged person."

"Mycroft, I am disappointed. Mental derangement is not a satisfactory explanation for such an act."

"Insane persons do insane things, Sherlock."

"In view of what I told you about the plot against President Hayes a year ago, how can you accept the preposterous explanation that this assassin is merely a deranged man?"

"You see a connection between that matter in New York last year and this act?"

"The assassin! What of him? What do you know?"

"His name is Guiteau. He shouted as he shot the President, 'I am a Stalwart! Arthur will be President!'"

Sherlock Holmes blanched and sank into a chair, his face buried in his hands. "What a tragedy! What a tragedy that I let that man slip through my hands."

Mycroft leaned forward, his great weight causing the big chair to creak in protest. "What do you mean, Sherlock?"

Holmes looked up at his brother. "Guiteau? His given name is Charles?"

Mycroft, whom Holmes had never known to be taken by surprise, jumped in shock. "Yes!"

"Charles Guiteau. The elusive Charles. The initials on that scrap of paper in Tebbel's pocket! C. G.," groaned Holmes.

Aware, now, of the importance of what his brother was saying, Mycroft whispered, "The fellow who escaped you on the Brooklyn Bridge was this same Charles Guiteau?"

With a forlorn shrug, Holmes replied, "Beyond question. And now he has succeeded with Garfield that which he and his dastardly bunch failed to do in the case of Hayes."

"A failure to kill Hayes, I point out to you, Sherlock, which was due to your excellent work in that case."

"But Charles escaped and see what he has done!"

Mycroft Holmes had no response.

President James A. Garfield lingered for more than two months, his physicians unable to locate the bullet fired by Guiteau. (It would be more than a dozen years until X rays.) Garfield died at his seaside cottage at Elberon, New Jersey, September 19, 1881, where he had been taken to escape the oppressive heat of Washington, D.C.

Succeeding to the Presidency, Chester A. Arthur took the oath of office in a tiny house on Lexington Avenue in New York City, only a few blocks from the spot where Nigel Tebbel had been slain on July 2, 1880. Never elected to public office in his own right (except the Vice-Presidency, which was automatic with the election of Garfield), Arthur was viewed as the epitome of all that is bad in the worst possible definition of the word 'politician.' Chester A. Arthur, 'The Gentleman Boss' of the New York Republican party and the darling of the Stalwarts, was the second Vice-President to attain that office as the result of an assassin's bullet.

Assassin Charles J. Guiteau was hanged.

At his trial it was decided that Guiteau was not acting as part of a conspiracy by the Stalwarts.

As did Mycroft Holmes, the overwhelming majority of those who investigated the Garfield murder and who questioned Guiteau insisted that he had acted alone and was insane, driven by a distorted sense of his own mission in life and his own importance. It is casually stated in most histories that Guiteau was a "disgruntled office-seeker," but he was a far more complexly motivated character than that. He admitted that he had stalked Garfield for at least six weeks prior to the attack upon him on July 2, 1881, with the intention of making 'Stalwart' Arthur the President by killing Garfield.

Although his statements after his arrest were regarded as lunatic ravings, Guiteau insisted that he acted on behalf of the Stalwarts. "I guess you have not talked with the Stalwarts," he told a newspaper interviewer. "The Stalwarts will protect me." He stated, "His death

[Garfield's] was a political necessity. I am a Stalwart of the Stalwarts."

The *Times* described Guiteau as a "half-crazed, pettifogging lawyer."

Who was Guiteau?

Could he have been part of a conspiracy?

Could that conspiracy have existed as early as July 2, 1880, and been directed at that time against Rutherford B. Hayes?

Julius Charles Guiteau was born in Freeport, Illinois, on September 8, 1841, of French-Canadian stock. He later transposed his names and called himself Charles. He spent some time at the University of Michigan, was smitten by the ideas of the Oneida Community, and harboured a variety of unusual religious notions. He earned a law degree and was admitted to the Chicago bar, but he had a poor reputation as a counsellor and left behind wherever he went a trail of unpaid debts and bad cheques. He lived by his wits and roamed around the eastern United States during the 1870s, domiciled in Boston and New York, and practicing law in New York from offices in Liberty Street.

Guiteau attached himself devotedly to the Republican party and the Stalwarts. In the aftermath of the Garfield assassination, former President Grant recalled, "While I was at the Fifth Avenue Hotel, just after the close of the Hayes campaign, this man Guiteau stopped there, too." Grant went on to remember Guiteau barging into his suite, although Grant had sent word that he wanted nothing to do with Guiteau. (Grant had been told Guiteau was a bother, some hanger-on by Grant's son.) Other New York Republicans remembered running into Guiteau on numerous occasions.

If one is to share Holmes' conviction that Guiteau was the elusive Charles of "The Adventure of the Stalwart Companions," it must be shown that Guiteau was, in fact, in New York City at the time of the plot against Hayes, that is, July 2, 1880.

He was.

In its extensive coverage of the events surrounding the Garfield assassination, *The New York Times* reported an interview with Emory A. Storrs, an influential Republican of the period, who remembered Guiteau. "I have met him in New York occasionally when he was there haunting the hotels, and last summer [1880] I saw him at the National Committee, rooms."

There is no better evidence than that of a reliable eyewitness, so this testimony by Storrs eliminates any doubt that Guiteau was at Republican National Committee meetings at the Fifth Avenue Hotel during the first days of July 1880 when the plot against Hayes was set in motion.

While it is assumed that Holmes eventually made the connection between Guiteau and the Charles who eluded capture on the Brooklyn Bridge in 1880, and while it may be assumed that the shrewd Hargreave would also discern a connection, there is no evidence that Roosevelt came to such a realisation, but if Holmes and Hargreave saw a connection, why did they not come forward to at least raise the question of whether Guiteau had been involved in a Stalwart plot against Hayes?

While aware of Holmes' advice against coming to conclusions without supporting data. I believe that the detectives hesitated to suggest that President Arthur came to power as a result of a conspiracy when it seemed improbable that Arthur had a connection with the Stalwart conspirators or Guiteau. Both detectives were aware what a traumatic experience it would have been for a nation which had only begun to recover from the Civil War and the Lincoln assassination to have laid upon it allegations of political treachery in the murder of Garfield. In short, it is easy to see how Holmes at Baker Street would elect to spare 'the noble democracy' the agony that publicising the Hayes affair would mean, especially in view of the fact that – to the surprise of everyone –

'Chet' Arthur was turning into a good President with not even a hint of personal scandal. That Holmes and Hargreave held their tongues I therefore attribute to patriotism – Hargreave's patriotic fervour for his native land, Holmes' to a country that was also, in his heart, his.

Notes

In these notes, I have endeavoured to show by reference to Watson's writings and through my own independent research the authenticity of the material which is included in the Roosevelt manuscript. My sources in my independent work include: *The New York Times; Theodore Roosevelt: An Autobiography*, Charles Scribner's Sons, New York, 1920; *The Complete Sherlock Holmes*, a single-volume compendium of the four novels and fifty-six adventures, published by Doubleday & Company, Inc., Garden City, New York; *Sherlock Holmes of Baker Street: A Life of the World's First Consulting Detective*, William S. Baring-Gould, Bramhall House, New York, 1962; *The Private Life of Sherlock Holmes*, Vincent Starrett, the Macmillan Co., New York, 1933, revised and enlarged by the University of Chicago Press, 1960.

CHAPTER ONE

Much of the autobiographical material which Roosevelt included in the opening passage of this chapter is echoed in Roosevelt's autobiography published in 1920 by Scribner's, indicating that Roosevelt may have referred for its writing to his notes prepared for "The Adventure of the Stalwart Companions." It is significant that Roosevelt, when preparing his autobiography, felt impelled to continue to observe Holmes' admonition that no part of the Gramercy Park affair be published in their lifetimes.

A recent search of the Harvard library has failed to uncover any copy of Holmes' tobacco monograph to which Roosevelt refers, indicating its loss through accident or oversight. Another possibility is that the monograph was purlointed by a student or teacher, a priceless addition to any collection of Sherlockiana, certainly.

Holmes' statement that "from a drop of water a logician could infer the possibility of an Atlantic or a Niagara without having seen or heard of one or the other" along with a lengthy dissertation upon the Art of Deduction appeared later in an article entitled "The Book of Life," which Dr Watson, after reading it, dismissed as "ineffable twaddle" until Holmes announced, "As for the article, I wrote it myself." ("A Study in Scarlet") The existence of this article has long been an object of intense search. To date, it has not been found and we are left with only the quotations from it in "A Study in Scarlet" and, now, in this publication of Holmes' theory voiced in conversation with Roosevelt, years before Watson quoted it.

The New York theatrical season in 1880 was, usually, November to May, indicating that the Sasanoff Company was such a respected ensemble that an off-season run could command full houses.

Roosevelt's whimsical decision to bring together two detectives without telling either about the other is a rich insight into the sense of humour and good nature of Roosevelt, attested to by those who knew him all his life. For a question raised by this meeting between Holmes and Hargreave, see the Notes on Chapter 3.

CHAPTER TWO

President Rutherford B. Hayes paid a private visit to New York City after having been the commencement speaker at Yale, arriving in New York at noon on July 2. That Hargreave would have been nervous about a seemingly routine visit by the President may be attributed to the widely circulated rumour ten days earlier that Hayes had died, a rumor that became so widespread that it was noted as a news item in *The New York Times* of June 23, 1880, nine days before Hayes' arrival in Hargreave's territory. It may well have been confidential information concerning this death report that had put the New York police on guard, given Hayes's unpopularity amount certain hotheaded political factions at the time. Yet Hargreave's amazement at Holmes' uncovering of the plot by the Stalwarts against Hayes indicates that Hargreave, at least, had no evidence that Hayes' life was in danger at this time and that the security precautions were routine.

It is interesting to note that even at the young age of twenty-two Roosevelt already held beliefs that were to mark his public life – that the privileged classes bore a special responsibility to set a moral tone for the nation, telling Hargreave that it is not the common man who damages society but wealthy members of American society when they leave scruples aside.

The references to the weather at this time lend validity to Roosevelt as the author of this remarkable document. July 2, 1880, was, in fact, a rainy day.

The rapid expansion of Manhattan 'uptown' as noted by Roosevelt's description of the 'Rialto' section below Forty-second Street is evidence that Roosevelt was very much concerned about the deterioration of the city of his birth as evidenced by the worsening morality he saw all around him, a development he deplored throughout his life and which he tried to do something about when he was Police Commissioner, attacking, particularly, the sordid people and life-styles flourishing around Manhattan's saloons.

CHAPTER THREE

The progress of the building of the Brooklyn Bridge was a matter of fascination for all New Yorkers. A wonder of engineering and American know-how, the great bridge was, at this time, three years from completion.

President Ulysses S. Grant had rewarded the faithful Chester A. Arthur in 1871 with appointment as Collector of the Port of New York, then the most important federal job in New York City because it controlled more than one thousand employees of the Customs House, every job a ripe political plum. For eight years, Arthur used this position to build his own political base and, it is alleged, to line his own pockets. Hayes removed Arthur from the post in 1879 in his efforts to rid the civil service of politics. It was a political dismissal deeply resented by some Republicans and one more reason for them to deny Hayes a chance for a second term. This anger at Hayes must have been, as Roosevelt supposes, a weighty matter on Hargreave's mind during Hayes' visit to the city.

The location of Holmes' dressing room "in steerage" was not unusual. Actors suffered generally at the hands of producers and theater owners, then as now.

Roosevelt's account of Holmes meeting Hargreave is at odds with the excellent biography of Holmes by Baring-Gould, who writes that Holmes and Hargreave collaborated in the case of "Vanderbilt and the Yeggman" in January 1880. Of course, when Baring-Gould wrote his biography he did not have access to the Roosevelt manuscript published here for the first time. That Holmes and Hargreave continued their professional relationship is beyond question. In "The Adventure of the

Dancing Men" Holmes remarks, "I therefore cabled to my friend, Wilson Hargreave, of the New York Police Bureau, who has more than once made use of my knowledge of London crime."

Holmes' reference to the *Harper's Magazine* article on the book by Noah K. Davis indicates, along with his subsequent references to the popular publications of the day, that Holmes was already the avid reader of the daily periodicals we find in Watson's stories. Holmes' demonstration of an intimate knowledge of the existence of New York's homeless newsboys also points up his passion for collecting papers to obtain the crime news that clogged the columns of New York's penny papers, flourishing by the score at this time. Roosevelt's observation of the clutter of Holmes' rooms at 39 East Twenty-second Street—stacks of newspapers everywhere – inevitably inspires comparisons to the clutter Watson deplored at 221B Baker Street, years later.

CHAPTER FOUR

The farewell for Edwin Booth at Delmonico's was unquestionably a notable social occasion, and the presence of Holmes, who may have been regarded as a two-bit actor by some, indicates he had entrée to high society. His previous connection with the Vanderbilts is apparently the reason for his familiarity with society. Holmes states that he was seated between the celebrated showman P. T. Barnum and Chief Justice Shea. Others at the affair, the *Times* reported, were Cyrus West Field and Joseph Jefferson. The breakfast was held on June 16, 1880. This conversation is interesting, as well, because it shows that Holmes did not meet Hargreave in the Vanderbilt case. Indeed, Hargreave is amazed to learn that one of the city's best families had been victimised by a crime. In keeping with his sense of confidentiality regarding his clients, Holmes does not mention that the case of which he speaks is that of "Vanderbilt and the Yeggman," but the solution of the crime accords with that described in Baring-Gould's biography. The after-dinner chat with Hargreave is pure Holmes, as anyone familiar with 'the canon' will recognise. Beginning with a bit of name-dropping. Holmes then discourses on one of his favorite subjects – tobacco, noting Hargreave has taken up smoking cigars wrapped in Sumatran leaf, which had been imported to the United States for the first time as a wrapper and filler in 1876. He mentions his tobacco monograph, the one which had impressed Roosevelt. Then he touches lightly on ways of identifying individuals by their tobacco ash, the shape of the ear, fingerprints, watches and bootlaces. (Holmes always paid close attention to individuality, of course, noting in "The Sign of Four" that you can never foretell what any one man will do, although "you can say with precision what an average number will be up to. Individuals vary, but percentages remain constant.") In "A Case of Identity" Holmes delivered a similar lecture on observing the commonplace: "I can never bring you to realise the importance of sleeves, the suggestiveness of thumbnails, or the great issues that may hang from a bootlace." Holmes sounds rather cold-blooded in his dismissal of emotion as a factor to be admitted into his personality when dealing with crime, but it was a lesson he learned painfully in those rare lapses when he permitted emotion to raise its head. In those instances, he usually ran into difficulties: "I assure you that the most winning woman I ever knew was hanged for poisoning three little children for their insurance-money," he laments in "The Sign of Four." In the same tale he warns, "Love is an emotional thing, and whatever is emotional is opposed to that true, cold reason, which I place above all things. I should never marry myself, lest I bias my judgment."

Here, as so often in the Watson writings, Holmes speaks passionately about his belief that the most commonplace crime is often the most mysterious because, as he states in "A Study in Scarlet," "it presents no new or special features from which deductions may be drawn."

It appears that Holmes, in his intervention in the Vanderbilt case, recommended that the culprit – the family footman – not be prosecuted, a decision probably based on a desire to keep the family's name out of the newspapers. How the Vanderbilts knew of Holmes and of his special abilities remains a mystery, especially in view of the fact, as indicated by Roosevelt's manuscript, that Holmes was not called into the case by Hargreave as suggested by Baring-Gould.

Gramercy Park was and is a fashionable address. Besides being the New York City home of Tilden, it was the address of Cyrus West Field, builder of the Atlantic Cable. A block away lived Peter Cooper, inventor and philanthropist and founder of the Cooper Union. As a frequent stroller in the neighborhood, Holmes surely visited these men. Holmes was living in a rooming house at 39 East Twenty-second Street. (The address is now encompassed by a larger apartment house.) Strolling around New York seems to have been Holmes' pastime when he was not acting. That he did not know that 15 Gramercy Park was Tilden's house underscores the fact that Holmes was not interested in politics and political personages except when they were involved in his cases. The Tilden house was really two houses remodelled into one large townhouse by architect Calvert Vaux, one of the famed designers of Central Park. After his election loss in 1876, Tilden spent much of his time out of the city at his country residence.

The restored Theodore Roosevelt house is maintained by the National Park Service and is open to visitors who may see the stately mansion as it was when Roosevelt was a youth.

Holmes often used the device of asking someone to comment on a fact that seemed obvious by its omission. In this case, the lack of powder marks. In another case, "Silver Blaze," Holmes has an exchange with a police inspector, who asks:

"Is there any point to which you wish to draw my attention?"

"To the curious incident of the dog in the night-time."

"The dog did nothing in the night-time."

"That was the curious incident," remarked Holmes.

In "The Adventure of the Noble Bachelor," Holmes again laments the effect of the American Revolution: "It is always a joy to me to meet an American... for I am one of those who believe that the folly of a monarch and the blundering of a minister in fargone years will not prevent our children from being some day citizens of the same world-wide country under a flag which shall be a quartering of the Union Jack with the Stars and Stripes."

CHAPTER FIVE

"No, no: I never guess. It is a shocking habit – destructive of the logical faculty," insists Holmes in "The Sign of Four," as frustrated in that later adventure as he appears in this one at the assertion by Hargreave that Holmes' abilities stemmed largely from guesswork.

Roosevelt, who had read Holmes' monograph on tobaccos, must have been amused to see Holmes, as a detective, seize upon the cigars as a vital clue in the case.

Holmes' lodgings appear to have been at 39 East Twenty-second Street for quite some time for him to have accumulated the things which Roosevelt describes, having moved to the boarding-house, one of many which flourished in the east twenties at this time, from the Union Square Hotel, mentioned previously by Roosevelt (Chapter 1: "... in a note from a hotel in Union Square..."). One imagines that the hotel management suggested to its guest that his smelly chemical experiments were disturbing the other guests!

Holmes' discussion of the architecture of New York, his knowledge of the chemistry of alloys, and his familiarity with the methods of breaking and entering indicate that in the years after he gave up formal education he had, indeed, spent his time studying anything and everything that the world's first consulting detective would need to know. His prediction that Manhattan island would give birth to high-rise buildings was made based on his familiarity with the introduction of steel skeleton construction and electricity – which made the elevator both necessary and possible, although it would be eight years before the Tower Building was put up at 50 Broadway on the design of Bradford Lee Gilbert, thus becoming Manhattan's first 'skyscraper.'

The identification of himself as William Escott to the newspaper reporter at the scene of the Tebbel murder shows again that Holmes wished to avoid having his name in the papers. This young newspaperman was, apparently, the writer of the item which set in motion the events that led to my discovery of Roosevelt's manuscript. His article was in error on one point: he wrote that Escott and Hargreave had been at dinner at Roosevelt's home when, as we know, they had been at the Hoffman House. In the conversation recorded by Roosevelt it is evident that the reporter was not told that Escott was an actor, so we may assume that he obtained that knowledge elsewhere in order to write that Escott was appearing in *Twelfth Night*. Perhaps the earnest young crime reporter also covered the theatrical beat, a not uncommon occurrence in the era of American journalism before the invention of that journalistic specialist – the dramatic critic.

Even the most casual reader of Holmes literature knows of Holmes' dabbling in cocaine. "Which is it today?" Watson asked in "The Sign of Four." "Morphine or cocaine?" It was cocaine, Holmes admitted. "A seven per-cent solution." To which Watson delivered a lecture on the evils of the snowy powder which Watson believed would "risk the loss of those great powers" which Holmes had spent his life developing.

There is no way of knowing from Roosevelt's manuscript if Holmes was already a user of cocaine in 1880 or simply a student of it.

CHAPTER SIX

Father John Christopher Drumgoole devoted himself to the plight of homeless and wayward children, supporting the work of his growing home for newsboys by publishing his own newspaper, *The Homeless Child*, beginning in 1883. Later, Drumgoole founded Mount Loretto on Staten Island, one of America's largest childcare institutions. While he worked hard for Mount Loretto, he did not abandon his interest in the newsboys' home, visiting it daily. However, in the Great Blizzard of 1888, when Father Drumgoole attempted to reach Manhattan, he contracted pneumonia. He died two weeks later at the age of seventy-two. The good people of New York remembered him by naming a boulevard for him on Staten Island. Obviously, Holmes' experience in recruiting an army of 'irregulars' from Father Drumgoole's newsboys proved a useful device which Holmes adopted successfully in later years in the form of the Baker Street Irregulars, led by the indomitable Wiggins.

It seems obvious that Roosevelt's exposure to the corruption and vice of New York's saloons, including those that catered to children, was uppermost in his mind as Police Commissioner in 1895 when he launched a campaign against the saloon businesses in New York City.

The resourceful Wakefield of this tale must, of course, be compared to the remarkable Wiggins of the Baker Street Irregulars who are prominent in the resolution of cases in "The Sign of Four" and "A Study in Scarlet," where Watson wrote, "The spokesman of the street arabs, young Wiggins, introduced his insignificant and unsavoury person." It is a most uncharitable way for Watson to refer to a lad who was obviously of great help to Holmes, and it is amusing to wonder if Watson might not have been a little jealous of others – especially a boy

– assisting Holmes with his problems. In pursuing whether Wakefield ultimately followed Holmes' advice and entered upon a career in the police, the author has made an exhaustive study of the rolls of the NYPD for the decade of the 1880s but to no avail. Wakefield appears to have faded into the same obscurity as Wiggins, although each of the lads has attained immortality by being part of the chronicles of the sleuth of Baker Street! For details on what was located at 24 State Street, see the Notes on Chapter 9.

CHAPTER SEVEN

The Five Points district, located, roughly speaking, between Park Row, Centre Street, and Grand Street (in the vicinity of the modern Chinatown), was very much like the Seven Dials of London. The area took its name from the intersections of streets and was but one of a number of very rough neighbourhoods of New York City in the latter half of the nineteenth century. These sections had wonderfully exciting names: Satan's Circus, the Tenderloin area that blossomed between Broadway and Ninth between Twenty-third and Forty-second streets; The Bowery, the mainstay of lower East Side gangsters; the Gashouse District, which got its name from the huge round gas storage tanks, in the east thirties; and the West Side's notorious Hell's Kitchen, just west of the Tenderloin. In the 1893 publication of *Baedeker's United States*, travellers were warned of these rough neighbourhoods and were cautioned at one point not to visit Chinatown unless accompanied by a detective. Each of these neighbourhoods contained the tenements and slums to which immigrants were relegated. Immigrants were cheap labour for the industrial concerns that flourished beside the rivers of the East and West sides of Manhattan.

In a speech at Durham, North Carolina, on October 19, 1905, Roosevelt, discoursing on courage, said, "Good weapons are necessary, but if you put the best weapon that can be invented in the hands of a coward, he will be beaten by a brave man with a club." In another address he spoke of the need for citizens who would "fight valiantly alike against the foes of the soul and the foes of the body," indicating that Roosevelt deeply believed – as did Holmes – that the fight against crime was not to be won unless men first achieved a victory over moral corruption.

In "The Sign of Four," Holmes again mused on the "little immortal spark" concealed in every man, no matter what sort of rascal he might be, and, in "The Retired Colourman," Holmes says, "Is not all life pathetic and futile?" Holmes was to express the same thought in "The Cardboard Box" as Watson pondered the meaning of misery: "What is the meaning of it, Watson? What object is served by this circle of misery and violence and fear? It must tend to some end, or else our universe is ruled by chance, which is unthinkable. But what end? There is the great standing perennial problem to which human reason is as far from an answer as ever."

Holmes discourses on the rose as evidence of the goodness of Providence, again, in "The Naval Treaty."

Holmes expounded his theory about sin in the city as compared to that in the country in "The Copper Beeches," an adventure played out in the most beautiful of countrysides. "It is my belief, Watson, founded upon my experience, that the lowest and vilest of alleys in London do not present a more dreadful record of sin than does the smiling and beautiful countryside... the pressure of public opinion can do in the town what the law cannot accomplish. There is no lane so vile that the scream of a tortured child, or the thud of a drunkard's blow, does not beget sympathy and indignation among the neighbours, and then the whole machinery of justice is ever so close that a word of complaint can set it going, and there is but a step between the crime and the dock. But look at these lonely houses, each in its own fields, filled for the most part with poor, ignorant folk who know little of the law.

Think of the deeds of hellish cruelty, the hidden wickedness which may go on, year in, year out, in such places, and none the wiser," Holmes said.

Holmes' maxim on the effect of appearances appears in a somewhat different form in "A Study in Scarlet" as Holmes observes that what you do in this world is a matter of little consequence. Rather, he states, the question is, "What you can make people believe that you have done."

It is hardly surprising that Holmes would notice Griggs' tattoo and be able to identify it even though he saw only a portion of it beneath Griggs' sleeve cuff. In "The Red-headed League," Holmes remarks to Mr. Jabez Wilson, "The fish that you have tattooed immediately above your right wrist could only have been done in China. I have made a small study of tattoo marks and have even contributed to the literature of the subject." This monograph on the subject of tattoos appears to be lost to us, but it seems likely, in view of this Roosevelt manuscript, that Holmes had made the study of tattoos prior to 1880 and that the monograph probably was published around the same time as the publications of his monographs on tobacco, the identification of footprints and the dating of documents.

Holmes frequently exhibited a familiarity with the American Civil War, an event that was to find mention in his subsequent cases, "The Five Orange Pips," "The Valley of Fear" and "The Cardboard Box."

CHAPTER EIGHT

Roosevelt's discourse on the realities of American politics accords with his subsequent writings on the system in which he was to play a part throughout his life. While Roosevelt deplored the sordid sides of big-city political machines, he was careful to defend their positive contributions. "The terms machine and machine politician are now undoubtedly used ordinarily in a reproachful sense," he wrote in *The Century*, November 1886, "but it does not at all follow that this sense is always the right one. On the contrary, the machine is often a very powerful instrument for good; and a machine politician really desirous of doing honest work on behalf of the community is fifty times as useful as is the average philanthropic outsider."

Theodore Roosevelt's confidence that no one would ever be elected to a third term as President finally proved unfounded when a member of his own family – his cousin, Franklin Delano Roosevelt – sought and won a third term in 1940 and a fourth in 1944, after which a Constitutional Amendment made Washington's concept of a two-term limit the law of the land.

CHAPTER NINE

The scene in which Roosevelt sits down at his desk and strikes a 'balance sheet' in the Tebbel case seems to mark the point at which Roosevelt is bitten by the 'detective bug,' although it would be fifteen years before he became President of the Board of Police Commissioners of the New York Police Department. A word about that service may be appropriate. Until 1895, Roosevelt had been serving with great distinction as a member of the Civil Service Commission, appointed to the post in 1889 by President Harrison. In that period, Civil Service rules were extended to more than fifty thousand government employees. Meanwhile in New York City, a coalition of political parties formed in 1894 to oppose Tammany Hall, electing W. L. Strong as mayor. Strong first asked Roosevelt to head the Street Cleaning Department and Roosevelt declined. He accepted the job as head of the Police Department and placed the historically corrupt force on a thoroughly efficient basis. His major accomplishment was to put an end to the despicable habit of members of the Police Department blackmailing victims encountered in the course of duty. Roosevelt took over in 1895, a date which coincides with the so-called missing year in the biography of Sherlock Holmes, leading to speculation – and it must be speculation, because there is no supporting evidence – that Holmes had returned to New York to be of assistance to Roosevelt in reorganising the police. Baring-Gould indicates that it was in the period of late 1895 to late 1896 that Holmes cleared his brother Sherrinford of the charge of murder, "an investigation that led him in turn to a cesspool of ancient horrors associated with black magic," but Holmes' exact activities and whereabouts in this year are the subject of speculation only, and it is to this speculative realm that we must assign the tantalising prospect that Holmes helped clean up corruption in the NYPD.

As in London, it was commonplace for New Yorkers to use the services of scores of private messenger services, as well as the telegraph office, for crosstown communications in the era before telephones. Holmes' message to Hargreave probably was sent through one of these private services available in all of the hotels in the area around his lodgings on Twenty-second Street.

By now, anyone who has even a passing acquaintance with Sherlock Holmes knows of his extraordinary knack for makeup and costumes, learned during his association with the Sasanoff troupe and put to such remarkable use in various adventures. However, it was not until another consummate actor and master of makeup brought Sherlock Holmes to the movie screen that admirers of Holmes were able to see the magical transformations Holmes effected – the actor Basil Rathbone. In one of Rathbone's 'Holmes' films, the actor, in pursuit of Moriarty, donned much the same disguise as that described herein by Roosevelt – sailor's cap, shirt, and dungarees, though without the beard. One of Rathbone's most effective 'Holmes disguises' was that of an English music hall performer in the film *The Adventures of Sherlock Holmes.* Holmes' off-hand reference herein to his disguise as "a little old flower-lady who would win your hearts" is too tempting to contemplate!

Holmes' little discourse on his reasoning process accords with that of a similar one in "The Five Orange Pips." Holmes states, "The ideal reasoner would, when he has once been shown a single fact in all its bearings, deduce from it not only all the chain of events which led up to it, but also all the results which would follow from it. As Cuvier could correctly describe a whole animal by the contemplation of a single bone, so the observer who has thoroughly understood one link in a series of incidents should be able to accurately state all the other ones, both before and after." Something which Holmes proceeded to do brilliantly in deducing that the murder of Nigel Tebbel was part of a plot to assassinate President Hayes. Yet Holmes seems bothered by his readiness to "jump to a conclusion," even a correct one. As he remarks later in "A Scandal in Bohemia," it is "a capital mistake to theorise before one has data."

The *Times* reports that President Hayes dined aboard the S.S. *Mosel* with Herr Schumacher; Postmaster General Key; Governor Howard of Rhode Island; U.S. Attorney Woodford and his wife; and Captain Neynaber of the *Mosel,* who would be commanding the splendid oceanliner as she left her dock at Hoboken, New Jersey, on Saturday, July 3. North German Lloyds vessels usually sailed on Saturdays. Hayes left New York in the afternoon of July 3 after spending the day safely at the Woodford residence at Manhattan Beach. The news accounts of the visit contain no mention of any plot against Hayes, a tribute to the skill with which Holmes handled this delicate situation.

The British Consul General's office was located at 24 State Street, and it was an urgent message to the Consul General which Wakefield carried the previous night at Holmes' behest. It might have been assumed that the British envoy would have been a friend of Mycroft Holmes, who was associated with the British government in various capacities. It is quite surprising to learn that Holmes knew the British Consul General from a date when they had been students under the mathematics tutelage of none other than Professor James Moriarty! In later adventures, Professor Moriarty would be described by Holmes as "the Napoleon of crime" and organiser of half that is evil and nearly all that is undetected; a genius, a philosopher, an abstract thinker. Odd, that Holmes – a genius, a philosopher, and an abstract thinker, himself – would describe Moriarty in this adventure as a man he didn't like when they ought to have hit it off wonderfully, having so much in common. Or, did Holmes instinctively know even at this early date that Moriarty was the personification of crime and that they were destined to have a deadly struggle?

Holmes describes his commandeering of a local policeman as an extraordinary act, but he was to make it commonplace for himself in the years to come!

CHAPTER TEN

Nothing in the literature of crime matches for sheer thrill the picture of Sherlock Holmes on the scent, dashing to various parts of a city in search of the persons who may put into his hands the ends of the minute strands of evidence and circumstance that will lead him to the resolution of his 'problem.' In this instance, beginning with visits to tobacco wholesale markets in order to trace Tebbel's cigar and then to the Customs House for data on the berths of German steamships, finally comparing this data and pinpointing the spot where a dastardly crime might be committed. Holmes lectures Watson on his investigative process in "The Disappearance of Lady Frances Carfax." He points out, "When you follow two separate chains of thought, Watson, you will find some point of intersection which should approximate the truth."

It seems probable that the hotel where the conspirators waited without success for a chance to kill President Hayes stood on West Street where it meets Christopher and Barrow streets, the Manhattan terminus of the Hoboken ferry most likely used to convey passengers to the Hoboken pier of the German steamship company.

Holmes was not ashamed to boast of his talents as a burglar. "You know, Watson, I don't mind confessing to you that I have always had an idea that I would have made a highly efficient criminal," he states in "Charles Augustus Milverton," producing for Watson's perusal a "first-class, up-to-date burgling kit, with nickel-plated jemmy, diamond-tipped glass cutter, adaptable keys, and every modern improvement which the march of modern civilisation demands."

Holmes' performance in reconstructing what transpired in room 405 of the hotel on West Street during the night of July 2–3, 1880, is a typical example of the Holmes method: "It has long been an axiom of mine that the little things are infinitely the most important" ("A Case of Identity").

"The faculty of deduction is certainly contagious, Watson," exclaims Holmes in "Thor Bridge," complimenting Watson for an achievement, just as he complimented Roosevelt in this adventure.

The Broadway Squad was a nineteenth-century forerunner of the special task forces which the New York Police Department would use, ranging from undercover decoy cops posing as drunks, old women, and handicapped persons to lure muggers to the special task force that included more than one hundred detectives in the search for the "Son of Sam." The Broadway Squad had been set up primarily to protect theatregoers in the 'Rialto' that stretched from Union Square to Forty-second Street. These were hand-picked men (described by Roosevelt in Chapter 3) and were, as Holmes dubs them, New York's "finest." The job of these plainclothes street cops was made somewhat easier in 1880 by the installation of lights on Broadway from Fourteenth Street to Twenty-sixth, but as any cop of the Times Square beat today will tell you, the worst possible crimes are committed beneath the brightest of lights.

CHAPTER ELEVEN

The Tilden House at 15 Gramercy Park South is now the home of the National Arts Club, founded in 1898, which took over the Tilden mansion for its headquarters in 1906. Roosevelt returned to the address after he retired from the White House, lunching daily in the club's dining room and conducting meetings connected with his editorship of *The Outlook*. The National Arts Club was the second private club to move into what had been an exclusive residential community. The Players, founded by Edwin Booth, opened a few years earlier next door to the Tilden house. If, in fact, Holmes came back to New York City in the 'missing year' of 1895–96, it seems likely that he would have visited The Players, although he may have used his stage name, Escott.

After his defeat under the peculiar circumstances of the 1876 Presidential election, Tilden preferred to live as private a life as possible, eventually giving up his Gramercy Park residence in favour of his Yonkers estate. Gramercy Park was founded as a private park and remains one to this day, keys to its gates available only to those who live in the homes surrounding it. (The original keys were gold.)

Theodore Roosevelt married Alice Lee on October 27, 1880, his twenty-second birthday, the marriage taking place in Boston. Alice Lee Roosevelt was a nineteen-year-old blue-eyed, brown-haired beauty. The couple returned to Manhattan where Roosevelt attended Columbia Law School in the winter of 1880–81. Roosevelt did not enjoy the study of law and gave it up, taking his bride to Europe in the summer of 1881.

There, he collected information for a book he had begun at Harvard, *The Naval War of 1812*. It seems likely that Roosevelt would have dropped in on Sherlock Holmes to introduce the sleuth to the new Mrs Roosevelt. Holmes, it seems probable, would have introduced the Roosevelts to his new roommate, Dr John H. Watson, whom Holmes had met in January 1881. That Roosevelt corresponded with Watson (as evidenced by the documents cited in the Introduction) proves conclusively that the two men had met before beginning their correspondence. It is probable that they met more than once. The second meeting would appear to have occurred in December 1886, when Roosevelt was again abroad (this time to marry his second wife – his first wife, Alice, having died in February 1884). On December 2, 1886, Dr Watson and Holmes would surely have attended Roosevelt's wedding to Edith Kermit Carow, a woman three years younger than himself but whom he had known since childhood. The third reunion of Roosevelt and Holmes was, as I have speculated, in 1895, when Holmes came to New York to assist Roosevelt in cleaning up the New York police department. Following is a representation of the pertinent dates in the lives of both men:

HOLMES	ROOSEVELT
Born, Jan. 6, 1854.	Born, Oct, 27, 1858.
Nov. 23, 1879. Sails for New York with Sasanoff troupe.	**Senior at Harvard.**
Jan. 1880. "Vanderbilt and the Yeggman."	
July 2, 1880. Performs as Malvolio in *Twelfth Night* at Union Square Theatre; New York.	**Attends *Twelfth Night* as guest of 'William Escott.'**

HOLMES *cont.*	**ROOSEVELT** *cont.*

July 2, 3, 1880: "The Adventure of the Stalwart Companions."

Late July 1880, the Abernetty family case in Baltimore.	**Leaves for vacation in the West with * brother, Elliott.**
Aug. 5, 1880. Returns to England.	
	Oct. 27, 1880. Marries Alice Hathaway Lee in Boston: Studies law at Columbia Law School.
Jan. 1881. Meets Dr. John H. Watson. They move to 221B Baker Street.	
	Summer 1881. Tours Europe with wife. Meets Dr Watson, introduced by Holmes.
1882. World's only private consulting detective.	1882–84. Member, New York State legislature.
	Jan. 1884. Death of wife, Alice.
	Oct. 1886. Defeated in bid for mayor of New York.
Dec. 2, 1886. Attends Roosevelt wedding, accompanied by Dr Watson.	**Dec. 2, 1886. Marries Edith Kermit Carow in a ceremony in London.**
May 4, 1891. Holmes is presumed killed in struggle with Prof. Moriarty at the Reichenbach Falls.	1891–95. Serves on U.S. Civil Service Commission.
July 1891. The first of Watson's short stories appears in *The Strand Magazine*.	
April 5, 1894. Holmes' 'return.'	
	July 1894. Roosevelt's correspondence with Holmes and Watson regarding

HOLMES *cont.*	ROOSEVELT *cont.*
	"The Adventure of the Stalwart Companions."
Late 1895–96. The 'missing year.' Was Holmes in New York assisting Roosevelt?	**1895–97. President, Board of Police Commissioners.**
1897–1957. Consulting detective.	
Died, Jan. 6, 1957, at the age of 103.	
	1901. Vice-President of the United States.
	1901–09. President of the United States.
	Died, Jan. 6, 1919, at the age of 61.

(A more detailed chronology of Holmes's life may be found in Baring-Gould's life of Holmes. Roosevelt wrote an autobiography.)

CHAPTER TWELVE

In 1880, as today, no one was a better observer, reporter, or commentator on the affairs, morals, and modes of the day than the cab driver! Although public mass transit was in its incipient stages in the city (there were elevated trains on the East and West sides and tramways), those who could afford it or who didn't want the jostle and bounce and crowding of the trains and cars could call on the hackneys and coaches that plied the streets and avenues. The astute observations of the doorman at the Union League Club indicate that then, as now, the city's doormen were every bit as observant as the cabbies.

The Republican National Committee met at the Fifth Avenue Hotel beginning July 1, 1880, to organise the Garfield-Arthur campaign, coming out of its meetings with the usual declarations of party solidarity and forecasts of an impending defeat of the Democratic slate. The party unity thus outwardly achieved was a result of compromises at the convention in June which put New York's Chester A. Arthur on the Garfield ticket. The Arthur nomination was largely the handiwork of party boss Senator Roscoe Conkling. Arthur was Conkling's protégé and was rewarded for his efforts for Grant in 1868 by appointment as Collector of the Port of New York, the rich patronage position from which Hayes dismissed Arthur in 1879 to the consternation of the Stalwarts. Upon the election of Garfield and Arthur, the Stalwarts expected Garfield to put New York patronage in the hands of a Stalwart. However, Garfield gave Arthur's old job as Collector to a 'Half-Breed' adherent of James G. Blaine, an act that was to have a significant impact on the solidarity heralded by the National Committee at their July 1880 meeting.

The first practical typewriting machine had been patented by the American journalist C. L. Sholes in 1867, and Holmes appears by his obvious familiarity with the machine to have made quite a study of it, with special attention to its value as a means of providing clues in criminal investigations. While he mentioned to Augustus Roosevelt his intention of writing a monograph on the subject, he still had not done so some years later. He stated in "A Case of Identity" that he was thinking "of writing another little monograph some of these days on the typewriter and its relation to crime. It is a subject to which I have devoted some little attention."

CHAPTER THIRTEEN

It appears that Roosevelt has given the central character of this conspiracy a fictitious name in preparing his manuscript. No record exists of any prominent person with the name Tiberius Gaius Nero Veil.

Obviously, Roosevelt took the names of four Caesars for this man's given names. The surname, Veil, is, apparently, an anagram of the word 'evil.' The political history which this man relates makes sense in terms of his Republican associations, but it is a history which fits numerous Republicans of the era. Nor is the familiarity with Arthur (calling him 'Chet,' for instance) a clue, because Arthur was known as 'Chet' to hundreds of political hacks.

There was definitely an incident of some kind involving Hayes at Columbus, Ohio, on June 22, 1880. A newspaper account dismisses it as a rumour in which Hayes was reported to have dropped dead on a street in the city while he was in Ohio to attend a college graduation.

Readers of Watson know that Holmes' landlady, Mrs Hudson, followed the English custom of preparing and serving Holmes meals, but the lodging and rooming houses of New York City in the year 1880 did not follow this practice. Holmes surely had to have had quite an impact on the Italian lady who rented him his rooms, but, alas, if the lady had harboured hopes of a romance with the young Englishman, she was bound to be disappointed, given Holmes' strong views on the pitfalls awaiting a detective who permitted romance to complicate his life.

The violin, like the deerstalker cap, Inverness cloak, pipe, and magnifying glass, has become indelibly identified with Holmes. He played a Stradivarius at 221B Baker Street, but the cavalier manner in which he handled the violin which Roosevelt describes, permitting it to be buried under the clutter of his Twenty-second Street rooms, indicates that Holmes had not yet acquired his 'Strad.' Again and again, in lulls during his cases or immediately after solving them, Holmes resorted to "violin-land, where all is sweetness, and delicacy, and harmony" ("The Redheaded League"). In "The Five Orange Pips," he tells Watson, "Hand me over my violin and let us try to forget for half an hour the

miserable weather, and the still more miserable ways of our fellow-men."
But Holmes' liking for music went beyond that which he produced
himself. He frequented numerous concerts in London. ("Let us escape
from this weary workaday world by the side door of music. Carina sings
tonight at the Albert Hall, and we still have time to dress, dine, and
enjoy," he says in "The Retired Colourman.") There were plenty of
chances to escape by the side door of music in 1880s New York. The
famous Academy of Music stood on Fourteenth Street, a short walk
from Holmes' rooms and on the same street as the Union Square
Theatre. Holmes could hear music by the New York Symphony
Orchestra or catch recitals at Steinway and Chickering halls. New York
City was opening its vistas to music from Britain, as well. Gilbert and
Sullivan had arrived in late 1879.

Holmes' disgust at suicide is evident in a number of the cases
recorded by Watson. In "The Veiled Lodger," Holmes addresses a
suicidal Eugenia Ronder. "Your life is not your own. Keep your hands
off it." He adds, "The example of patient suffering is in itself the most
precious of all lessons to an impatient world."

CHAPTER FOURTEEN

The original building which housed the Gilsey Hotel and the Silver
Dollar Bar still stands in New York, although the once-revolutionary
cast-iron facing has been allowed to deteriorate. Recently, a developer
announced plans to renovate the structure into an apartment house.

While Holmes seems to boast, here, that his special knowledge and
powers which encouraged him to seek complex explanations were an
asset, he seems to have some doubts in "The Abbey Grange" when he
laments having looked for something more complex when the simpler
solution was right before his eyes. How could he, he wonders, overlook
something as obvious as the half-empty bottle, the three wine glasses,

the curious fact that the lady was tied to a chair, and that she had had Australian origins and associations?

Characteristically, Holmes shuns public praise or notice of his work in preferring a personal memento of the case from Hargreave. That memento appears to have been something quite common for men engaged in arresting criminals – a pair of handcuffs. Holmes proudly showed them off to a man from Scotland Yard a few years after his collaboration with Hargreave.

CHAPTER FIFTEEN

One reads of the struggle with villainy on the Brooklyn Bridge with a sense of déjà vu, the mind racing forward eleven years to another precarious perch above swirling black waters – the Reichenbach Falls of Switzerland! There, in 1891, Sherlock Holmes was believed to have plunged to his death after a bitter struggle with "the Napoleon of crime," Professor Moriarty. Roosevelt must have learned of this apparent tragedy from Watson, who certainly would have informed him of it. Too, Roosevelt would have been ecstatic with joy on learning, in 1894, that Holmes had not been killed and that he had been wandering the world under the name of Sigerson. In the period between 1891 and 1894, Roosevelt followed the adventures of his friend Holmes in the regular appearances in *The Strand Magazine* of Watson's shorter accounts of Holmes' adventures. These publications, as we have seen, prompted Roosevelt to offer "The Adventure of the Stalwart Companions" for publication – only to be discouraged in that endeavour by Holmes himself.

CHAPTER SIXTEEN

It is hard not to look ahead from the scene in which Holmes and Roosevelt are basking in the afterglow of having completed a difficult case to see Holmes with Watson at his side, "a trusty companion." In less than a year after his collaboration with Roosevelt, Sherlock Holmes would be introduced to Dr John Watson, one of the most fortuitous and satisfying friendships in history, resulting in that great body of writing by which most of us have come to know Sherlock Holmes. Waxing philosophical with Roosevelt and musing about what strange things they might find if they could peer into the secrets of New York City, Holmes rehearses a speech expressing similar sentiments which he would direct to Watson in "A Case of Identity." To Watson, Holmes says, "My dear fellow, life is infinitely stranger than anything which the mind of man could invent."

A man who would always keep his commitments, Holmes, as homesick as he seems to be, shuns the suggestion that he abandon the Sasanoff tour and go home to London. From New York, he went to Baltimore where he solved the awful affair of the Abernetty family, resolving the case on the basis of his observation of the depth to which the parsley, had sunk into the butter. Holmes proved to be a devoted user of the phonograph, not only for his pleasure in listening to recorded music, but in his work. In the motion picture *The Voice of Terror*, Holmes discerns the existence of a Nazi spy in Britain by carefully calculating the differences in frequencies between a 'live' broadcast and a recorded one. It is instructive to note that as early as 1880 Holmes sees the possible usefulness of 'bugging,' wiretaps, and other clandestine recording as a police device.

Upon the discovery in this text that Holmes may have made a recording at the Edison laboratory in Menlo Park, B. Alexander 'Wiggy' Wiggins was beside himself with enthusiasm:

"My God, think of it! Think of the implications!" he cried, setting aside the last page of the Roosevelt manuscript, his eyes alight, his pudgy hands trembling. "If what Roosevelt wrote here is true, there existed at one point in time, a century ago, a recording of Sherlock Holmes' voice! Holmes recorded by Edison! The discovery of the century!"

Gently assembling the pages of "The Adventure of the Stalwart Companions," which we had finished reading in the archives of the New York Police Department, I reminded Wiggy that he had described the finding of the manuscript as the discovery of the century!

"Bah! These papers pale in comparison to an actual recording of Holmes' voice! I must find that recording!"

"Where are you going?" I asked as he pushed his huge body to its feet.

"Where am I going? Why, to Menlo Park! My search for the recording of Holmes' voice must start there!"

"But what about these documents?"

"You take care of them. Publish them!"

"But..."

"I have to find that recording."

"It can't possibly exist after all this time!"

"As long as there is a chance the recording exists. I have to make an effort to find it," he exclaimed as he turned and strode away, his huge body jiggling as the moved – far more rapidly than I might have imagined he could. He did not look back.

I have not seen Wiggy since that day, although I have heard of him showing up in the most unlikely locations from Menlo Park to London to Beirut to Shanghai, an improbable knight errant, a true believer in the 'canon,' traipsing the world in search of his personal Grail.

A Note...

By The Author On Veracity

Despite my efforts to demonstrate through independent research and verification the genuineness of this material, it will be alleged that all of the events, the documents, and the manuscript are the work of a clever hoaxer. If so, I am the chief victim. (My publisher has chosen the expedient of putting this book among its fiction list, you note – a decision which I have elected to accept in order to have this important discovery published!) A close friend who read this material while I was preparing it for publication suggested that if it were a hoax it could have been concocted only by a genius with such a thorough knowledge of Holmes as to be the world's greatest living expert on him. "A man such as your friend Wiggins," he suggested mischievously.

A hoax or the genuine article?

I believe this material is genuine. I believe my research indicates that it was possible for Holmes and Roosevelt to have known each other and to have collaborated in "The Adventure of the Stalwart Companions."

The reader, of course, must judge for himself.

I ask only that in reaching that judgment the reader will apply

Holmes' acid test for veracity: when you have eliminated the impossible, whatever remains, however improbable, must be the truth.

Also Available

the further adventures of SHERLOCK HOLMES

THE VEILED DETECTIVE

DAVID STUART DAVIES

Afghanistan,
The Evening Of 27 June 1880

The full moon hovered like a spectral observer over the British camp. The faint cries of the dying and wounded were carried by the warm night breeze out into the arid wastes beyond. John Walker staggered out of the hospital tent, his face begrimed with dried blood and sweat. For a moment he threw his head back and stared at the wide expanse of starless sky as if seeking an answer, an explanation. He had just lost another of his comrades. There were now at least six wounded men whom he had failed to save. He was losing count. And, by God, what was the point of counting in such small numbers anyway? Hundreds of British soldiers had died that day, slaughtered by the Afghan warriors. They had been outnumbered, outflanked and routed by the forces of Ayub Khan in that fatal battle at Maiwand. These cunning tribesmen had truly rubbed the Union Jack into the desert dust. Nearly a third of the company had fallen. It was only the reluctance of the Afghans to carry out further carnage that had prevented the British troops from being completely annihilated. Ayub Khan had his victory. He had made his point. Let the survivors report the news of his invincibility.

For the British, a ragged retreat was the only option. They withdrew into the desert, to lick their wounds and then to limp back to Candahar. They had had to leave their dead littering the bloody scrubland, soon to be prey to the vultures and vermin.

Walker was too tired, too sick to his stomach to feel anger, pain or frustration. All he knew was that when he trained to be a doctor, it had been for the purpose of saving lives. It was not to watch young men's pale, bloody faces grimace with pain and their eyes close gradually as life ebbed away from them, while he stood by, helpless, gazing at a gaping wound spilling out intestines.

He needed a drink. Ducking back into the tent, he grabbed his medical bag. There were still three wounded men lying on makeshift beds in there, but no amount of medical treatment could save them from the grim reaper. He felt guilty to be in their presence. He had instructed his orderly to administer large doses of laudanum to help numb the pain until the inevitable overtook them.

As Walker wandered to the edge of the tattered encampment, he encountered no other officer. Of course, there were very few left. Colonel MacDonald, who had been in charge, had been decapitated by an Afghan blade very early in the battle. Captain Alistair Thornton was now in charge of the ragged remnants of the company of the Berkshire regiment, and he was no doubt in his tent nursing his wound. He had been struck in the shoulder by a jezail bullet which had shattered the bone.

Just beyond the perimeter of the camp, Walker slumped down at the base of a skeletal tree, resting his back against the rough bark. Opening his medical bag, he extracted a bottle of brandy. Uncorking it, he sniffed the neck of the bottle, allowing the alcoholic fumes to drift up his nose. And then he hesitated.

Something deep within his conscience made him pause. Little did this tired army surgeon realise that he was facing a decisive moment of Fate. He was about to commit an act that would alter the course of his life for ever. With a frown, he shook the vague dark unformed thoughts from his mind and returned his attention to the bottle.

The tantalising fumes did their work. They promised comfort and oblivion. He lifted the neck of the bottle to his mouth and took a large gulp. Fire spilled down his throat and raced through his senses. Within moments he felt his body ease and relax, the inner tension melting with the warmth of the brandy. He took another gulp, and the effect increased. He had found an escape from the heat, the blood, the cries of pain and the scenes of slaughter. A blessed escape. He took another drink. Within twenty minutes the bottle was empty and John Walker was floating away on a pleasant, drunken dream. He was also floating away from the life he knew. He had cut himself adrift and was now heading for stormy, unchartered waters.

As consciousness slowly returned to him several hours later, he felt a sudden, sharp stabbing pain in his leg. It came again. And again. He forced his eyes open and bright sunlight seared in. Splinters of yellow light pierced his brain. He clamped his eyes shut, embracing the darkness once more. Again he felt the pain in his leg. This time, it was accompanied by a strident voice: "Walker! Wake up, damn you!"

He recognised the voice. It belonged to Captain Thornton. With some effort he opened his eyes again, but this time he did it more slowly, allowing the brightness to seep in gently so as not to blind him. He saw three figures standing before him, each silhouetted against the vivid blue sky of an Afghan dawn. One of them was kicking his leg viciously in an effort to rouse him.

"You despicable swine, Walker!" cried the middle figure, whose left arm was held in a blood-splattered sling. It was Thornton, his commanding officer.

Walker tried to get to his feet, but his body, still under the thrall of the alcohol, refused to co-operate.

"Get him up," said Thornton.

The two soldiers grabbed Walker and hauled him to his feet. With his good hand, Thornton thrust the empty brandy bottle before his face. For a moment, he thought the captain was going to hit him with it.

"Drunk on duty, Walker. No, by God, worse than that. Drunk while your fellow soldiers were in desperate need of your attention. You left them... left them to die while you... you went to get drunk. I should have you shot for this – but shooting is too good for you. I want you to live... to live with your guilt." Thornton spoke in tortured bursts, so great was his fury.

"There was nothing I could do for them," Walker tried to explain, but his words escaped in a thick and slurred manner. "Nothing I could–"

Thornton threw the bottle down into the sand. "You disgust me, Walker. You realise that this is a court martial offence, and believe me I shall make it my personal duty to see that you are disgraced and kicked out of the army."

Words failed Walker, but it began to sink in to his foggy mind that he had made a very big mistake – a life-changing mistake.

London, 4 October 1880

"Are you sure he can be trusted?" Arthur Sims sniffed and nodded towards the silhouetted figure at the end of the alleyway, standing under a flickering gas lamp.

Badger Johnson, so called because of the vivid white streak that ran through the centre of his dark thatch of hair, nodded and grinned.

"Yeah. He's a bit simple, but he'll be fine for what we want him for. And if he's any trouble…" He paused to retrieve a cut-throat razor from his inside pocket. The blade snapped open, and it swished through the air. "I'll just have to give him a bloody throat, won't I?"

Arthur Sims was not amused. "Where d'you find him?"

"Where d'you think? In The Black Swan. Don't you worry. I've seen him in there before — and I seen him do a bit of dipping. Very nifty he was, an' all. And he's done time. In Wandsworth. He's happy to be our crow for just five sovereigns."

"What did you tell him?"

"Hardly anything. What d'you take me for? Just said we were cracking a little crib in Hanson Lane and we needed a lookout. He's done the work before."

Sims sniffed again. "I'm not sure. You know as well as I do he ought to be vetted by the Man himself before we use him. If something goes wrong, we'll *all* have bloody throats… or worse."

Badger gurgled with merriment. "You scared, are you?"

"Cautious, that's all. This is a big job for us."

"And the pickin's will be very tasty, an' all, don't you worry. If it's cautious you're being, then you know it's in our best interest that we have a little crow keeping his beady eyes wide open. Never mind how much the Man has planned this little jaunt, *we're* the ones putting our heads in the noose."

Sims shuddered at the thought. "All right, you made your point. What's his name?"

"Jordan. Harry Jordan." Badger slipped his razor back into its special pocket and flipped out his watch. "Time to make our move."

Badger giggled as the key slipped neatly into the lock. "It's hardly criminal work if one can just walk in."

Arthur Sims gave his partner a shove. "Come on, get in," he whispered, and then he turned to the shadowy figure standing nearby. "OK, Jordan, you know the business."

Harry Jordan gave a mock salute.

Once inside the building, Badger lit the bull's-eye lantern and consulted the map. "The safe is in the office on the second floor at the far end, up a spiral staircase." He muttered the information, which he knew by heart anyway, as if to reassure himself now that theory had turned into practice.

The two men made their way through the silent premises, the thin yellow beam of the lamp carving a way through the darkness ahead of them. As the spidery metal of the staircase flashed into view, they spied an obstacle on the floor directly below it. The inert body of a bald-headed man.

Arthur Sims knelt by him. "Night watchman. Out like a light. Very special tea he's drunk tonight" Delicately, he lifted the man's eyelids to reveal the whites of his eyes. "He'll not bother us now, Badger. I reckon he'll wake up with a thundering headache around breakfast-time."

Badger giggled. It was all going according to plan.

Once up the staircase, the two men approached the room containing the safe. Again Badger produced the keyring from his pocket and slipped a key into the lock. The door swung open with ease. The bull's-eye soon located the imposing Smith-Anderson safe, a huge impenetrable iron contraption that stood defiantly in the far corner of the room. It was as tall as a man and weighed somewhere around three tons. The men knew from experience that the only way to get into this peter was by using the key – or rather the keys. There were five in all required. Certainly it would take a small army to move the giant safe, and God knows how much dynamite would be needed to blow it open, an act that would create enough noise to reach Scotland Yard itself.

Badger passed the bull's-eye to his confederate, who held the beam steady, centred on the great iron sarcophagus and the five locks. With another gurgle of pleasure, Badger dug deep into his trouser pocket and pulled out a brass ring containing five keys, all cut in a different manner. Scratched into the head of each key was a number – one that corresponded with the arrangement of locks on the safe.

Kneeling down in the centre of the beam, he slipped in the first key. It turned smoothly, with a decided click. So did the second. And the third. But the fourth refused to budge. Badger cast a worried glance at his confederate, but neither man spoke. Badger withdrew the key and tried again, with the same result. A thin sheen of sweat materialised on his brow. What the hell was wrong here? This certainly wasn't in the plan. The first three keys had been fine. He couldn't believe the Man had made a mistake. It was unheard of.

"Try the fifth key," whispered Arthur, who was equally perplexed and worried.

In the desperate need to take action of some kind, Badger obeyed. Remarkably, the fifth key slipped in easily and turned smoothly, with the same definite click as the first three. A flicker of hope rallied Badger's dampened spirits and he turned the handle of the safe. Nothing happened. It would not budge. He swore and sat back on his haunches. "What the hell now?"

"Try the fourth key again," came his partner's voice from the darkness.

Badger did as he was told and held his breath. The key fitted the aperture without problem. Now his hands were shaking and he paused, fearful of failure again.

"Come on, Badger."

He turned the key. At first there was some resistance, and then…
it moved. It revolved. It clicked.

"The bastards," exclaimed Arthur Sims in a harsh whisper.
"They've altered the arrangement of the locks so they can't be
opened in order. His nibs ain't sussed that out."

Badger was now on his feet and tugging at the large safe door.
"Blimey, it's a weight," he muttered, as the ponderous portal began to
move. "It's bigger than my old woman," he observed, his spirits
lightening again. The door creaked open with magisterial slowness. It
took Badger almost a minute of effort before the safe door was wide
open.

At last, Arthur Sims was able to direct the beam of the lantern to
illuminate the interior of the safe. When he had done so, his jaw
dropped and he let out a strangled gasp.

"What is it?" puffed Badger, sweat now streaming down his face.

"Take a look for yourself," came the reply.

As Badger pulled himself forward and peered round the corner of
the massive safe door, a second lantern beam joined theirs. "The
cupboard is bare, I am afraid."

The voice, clear, brittle and authoritative, came from behind them,
and both felons turned in unison to gaze at the speaker.

The bull's-eye spotlit a tall young man standing in the doorway, a
sardonic smile touching his thin lips. It was Harry Jordan. Or was it?
He was certainly dressed in the shabby checked suit that Jordan wore
– but where was the bulbous nose and large moustache?

"I am afraid the game is no longer afoot, gentlemen. I think the
phrase is, 'You've been caught red-handed.' Now, please do not make
any rash attempts to escape. The police are outside the building,

awaiting my signal."

Arthur Sims and Badger Johnson stared in dumbfounded amazement as the young man took a silver whistle from his jacket pocket and blew on it three times. The shrill sound reverberated in their ears.

Inspector Giles Lestrade of Scotland Yard cradled a tin mug of hot, sweet tea in his hands and smiled contentedly. "I reckon that was a pretty good night's work."

It was an hour later, after the arrest of Badger Johnson and Arthur Sims, and the inspector was ensconced in his cramped office back at the Yard.

The young man sitting opposite him, wearing a disreputable checked suit which had seen better days, did not respond. His silence took the smile from Lestrade's face and replaced it with a furrowed brow.

"You don't agree, Mr Holmes?"

The young man pursed his lips for a moment before replying. "In a manner of speaking, it has been a successful venture. You have two of the niftiest felons under lock and key, and saved the firm of Meredith and Co. the loss of a considerable amount of cash."

"Exactly." The smile returned.

"But there are still questions left unanswered."

"Such as?"

"How did our two friends come into the possession of the key to the building, to the office where the safe was housed – and the five all-important keys to the safe itself?"

"Does that really matter?"

"Indeed it does. It is vital that these questions are answered in order to clear up this matter fully. There was obviously an accomplice involved who obtained the keys and was responsible for drugging the night-watchman. Badger Johnson intimated as much when he engaged my services as lookout, but when I pressed him for further information, he clammed up like a zealous oyster."

Lestrade took a drink of the tea. "Now, you don't bother your head about such inconsequentialities. If there was another bloke involved, he certainly made himself scarce this evening and so it would be nigh on impossible to pin anything on him. No, we are very happy to have caught two of the sharpest petermen in London, thanks to your help, Mr Holmes. From now on, however, it is a job for the professionals."

The young man gave a gracious nod of the head as though in some vague acquiescence to the wisdom of the Scotland Yarder. In reality he thought that, while Lestrade was not quite a fool, he was blinkered to the ramifications of the attempted robbery, and too easily pleased at landing a couple of medium-size fish in his net, while the really big catch swam free. Crime was never quite as cut and dried as Lestrade and his fellow professionals seemed to think. That was why this young man knew that he could never work within the constraints of the organised force as a detective. While at present he was reasonably content to be a help to the police, his ambitions lay elsewhere.

For his own part, Lestrade was unsure what to make of this lean youth with piercing grey eyes and gaunt, hawk-like features that revealed little of what he was thinking. There was something cold and impenetrable about his personality that made the inspector feel uncomfortable. In the last six months, Holmes had brought several cases to the attention of the Yard which he or his fellow officer, Inspector Gregson, had followed up, and a number of arrests had resulted. What Sherlock Holmes achieved from his activities, apart from the satisfaction every good citizen would feel at either preventing or solving a crime, Lestrade could not fathom. Holmes never spoke of personal matters, and the inspector was never tempted to ask.

At the same time as this conversation was taking place in Scotland Yard, in another part of the city the Professor was being informed of the failure of that night's operation at Meredith and Co. by his number two, Colonel Sebastian Moran.

The Professor rose from his chaise-longue, cast aside the mathematical tome he had been studying and walked to the window. Pulling back the curtains, he gazed out on the river below him, its murky surface reflecting the silver of the moon.

"In itself, the matter is of little consequence," he said, in a dark, even voice. "Merely a flea-bite on the body of our organisation. But there have been rather too many of these flea-bites of late. They are now beginning to irritate me." He turned sharply, his eyes flashing with anger. "Where lies the incompetence?"

Moran was initially taken aback by so sudden a change in the Professor's demeanour. "I am not entirely sure," he stuttered.

The Professor's cruelly handsome face darkened with rage. "Well, you should be, Moran. You should be sure. It is your job to know. That is what you are paid for."

"Well… it seems that someone is tipping the police off in advance."

The Professor gave a derisory laugh. "Brilliant deduction, Moran. Your public-school education has stood you in good stead. Unfortunately, it does not take a genius to arrive at that rather obvious conclusion. I had a visit from Scoular earlier this evening, thank goodness there is *one* smart man on whom I can rely."

At the mention of Scoular's name, Moran blanched. Scoular was cunning, very sharp and very ambitious. This upstart was gradually worming his way into the Professor's confidence, assuming the role of court favourite; consequently, Moran felt his own position in jeopardy. He knew there was no demotion in the organisation. If you lost favour, you lost your life also.

"What did he want?"

"He wanted nothing other than to give me information regarding our irritant flea. Apparently, he has been using the persona of Harry Jordan. He's been working out of some of the East End alehouses, The Black Swan in particular, where he latches on to our more gullible agents, like Johnson and Sims, and then narks to the police."

"What's his angle?"

Moriarty shrugged. "I don't know – or at least Scoular doesn't know. We need to find out, don't we? Put Hawkins on to the matter. He's a bright spark and will know what to do. Apprise him of the situation and see what he can come up with. I've no doubt Mr Jordan will return to his lucrative nest at The Black Swan within the next few days. I want information only. This Jordan character must not be harmed. I just want to know all about him before I take any action. Do you think you can organise that without any slip-ups?"

Moran clenched his fists with anger and frustration. He shouldn't be spoken to in such a manner – like an inefficient corporal with muddy boots. He would dearly have liked to wipe that sarcastic smirk off the Professor's face, but he knew that such a rash action would be the ultimate folly.

"I'll get on to it immediately," he said briskly, and left the room.

The Professor chuckled to himself and turned back to the window. His own reflection stared back at him from the night-darkened pane. He was a tall man, with luxuriant black hair and angular features that would have been very attractive were it not for the cruel mouth and the cold, merciless grey eyes.

"Mr Jordan," he said, softly addressing his own reflection, "I am very intrigued by you. I hope it will not be too long before I welcome you into my parlour."

Dawn was just breaking as Sherlock Holmes made his weary way past the British Museum and into Montague Street, where he lodged. He was no longer dressed in the cheap suit that he had used in his persona as Harry Jordan, but while his own clothes were less ostentatious, they were no less shabby. Helping the police as he did was certainly broadening his experience of detective work, but it did not put bread and cheese on the table or pay the rent on his two cramped rooms. He longed for his own private investigation – one of real quality. Since coming to London from university to make his way in the world as a consulting detective, he had managed to attract some clients, but they had been few and far between, and the nature of the cases – an absent husband, the theft of a brooch, a disputed will, and such like – had all been mundane. But, tired as he was, and somewhat dismayed at the short-sightedness of his professional colleagues at Scotland Yard, he did not waver in his belief that one day he would reach his goal and have a solvent and successful detective practice. And it needed to be happening soon. He could not keep borrowing money from his brother, Mycroft, in order to fund his activities.

He entered 14 Montague Street and made his way up the three flights of stairs to his humble quarters. Once inside, with some urgency he threw off his jacket and rolled up the sleeve of his shirt. Crossing to the mantelpiece, he retrieved a small bottle and a hypodermic syringe from a morocco leather case. Breathing heavily with anticipation, he adjusted the delicate needle before thrusting the sharp point home into his sinewy forearm, which was already dotted and scarred with innumerable puncture marks. His long, white, nervous fingers depressed the piston, and he gave a cry of ecstasy as he flopped down in a battered armchair, a broad, vacant smile lighting upon his tired features.

THE FURTHER ADVENTURES OF SHERLOCK HOLMES
THE ECTOPLASMIC MAN

Daniel Stashower

When Harry Houdini is framed and jailed for espionage, Sherlock
Holmes vows to clear his name, with the two joining forces to take
on blackmailers who have targeted the Prince of Wales.
ISBN: 9781848564923

AVAILABLE NOW!

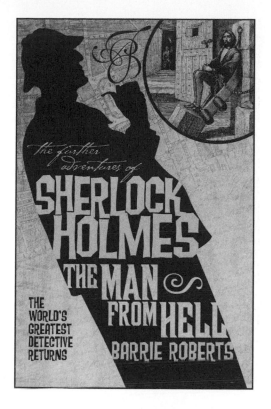

THE FURTHER ADVENTURES
OF SHERLOCK HOLMES

THE MAN FROM HELL

Barrie Roberts

In 1886, wealthy philathropist Lord Backwater is found beaten
to death on the grounds of his estate. Sherlock Holmes and Dr.
Watson must pit their wits against a ruthless new enemy...

ISBN: 9781848565081

AVAILABLE NOW!

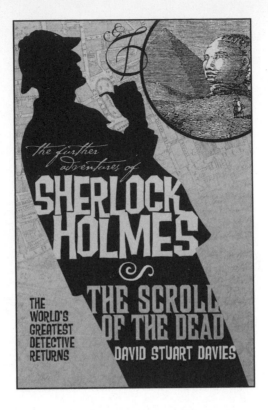

THE FURTHER ADVENTURES OF SHERLOCK HOLMES

THE SCROLL OF THE DEAD

David Stuart Davies

Holmes attends a seance to unmask an impostor posing as a
medium, Sebastian Melmoth, a man hell-bent on obtaining
immortality after the discovery of an ancient Egyptian papyrus. It
is up to Holmes and Watson to stop him and avert disaster...
ISBN: 9781848564930

AVAILABLE NOW!

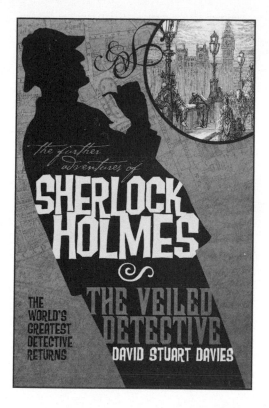

THE FURTHER ADVENTURES
OF SHERLOCK HOLMES
THE VEILED DETECTIVE

David Stuart Davies

A young Sherlock Holmes arrives in London to begin his career
as a private detective, catching the eye of the master criminal,
Professor James Moriarty. Enter Dr. Watson, newly returned
from Afghanistan, soon to make history as Holmes' companion...
ISBN: 9781848564909

AVAILABLE NOW!

THE FURTHER ADVENTURES
OF SHERLOCK HOLMES

THE WAR OF THE WORLDS

Manley Wade Wellman & Wade Wellman

Sherlock Holmes, Professor Challenger and Dr. Watson meet their
match when the streets of London are left decimated by a
prolonged alien attack. Who could be responsible for such
destruction? Sherlock Holmes is about to find out...
ISBN: 9781848564916

AVAILABLE NOW!

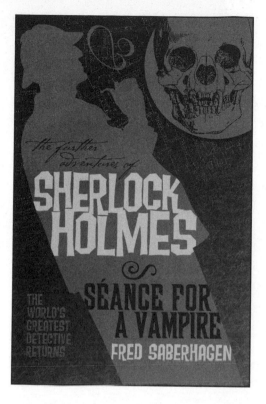

THE FURTHER ADVENTURES
OF SHERLOCK HOLMES
SEANCE FOR A VAMPIRE

Fred Saberhagen

When two psychics offer Ambrose Altamont the opportunity to contact his deceased daughter, Holmes is hired to expose their hoax. The result leaves one of the fraudulent spiritualists dead and Holmes missing. Watson has no choice but to summon the only one who might be able to help – Holmes' vampire cousin, Prince Dracula.
ISBN: 9781848566774

AVAILABLE JUNE 2010

THE FURTHER ADVENTURES
OF SHERLOCK HOLMES

THE SEVENTH BULLET

Daniel D. Victor

Sherlock Holmes' desire for a peaceful life in the Sussex
countryside is dashed when true-life muckraker and author David
Graham Phillips is assassinated. The pleas of his sister draws
Holmes and Watson to the far side of the Atlantic as they embark
on one of their most challenging cases.
ISBN: 9781848566767

AVAILABLE JUNE 2010